Trick
or
Murder?

DEBBIE YOUNG

COPYRIGHT PAGE

For David Penny for the Guy

"Everyone seems to have a clear idea
of how other people should lead their lives,
but none about his or her own."

Paulo Coelho

"Villagers should get to know
the newcomer better
before passing judgment."

Joshua Hampton

1 Strange Guys

On a crisp, bright autumn morning, an American tourist driving through the Cotswold village of Wendlebury Barrow pressed his foot down on the accelerator of his hired car. "Let's give it some gas and get out of here," he said to his wife. "What is this place anyway?"

"I don't know, honey, but I think we may have driven through a time warp. I just saw a sign advertising a fireworks party at the vicarage tonight. But this is November fifth, not July fourth."

She was cowering in the passenger seat at the sight of so many dead bodies being transported down the High Street. A young man was pushing one slumped in a wheelbarrow, while his friend carried another over his shoulder. A teenage girl had squeezed a third into a child's buggy. All were converging on the vicarage, where a small boy was currently dragging a body as big as himself across a muddy lawn littered with rotting windfall apples and dead leaves.

As the tourists drove by, they glimpsed a large mound of wood and paper at the centre of the back lawn. The woman gasped.

"Do you think that was a funeral pyre?"

"It's too late for a Halloween prank, whatever it was."

"Maybe they celebrate the Day of the Dead here?"

"No, that's Mexico." He passed her his phone. "Look up today's date and 'holidays' online, if you can get a signal in this godforsaken place."

The search engine's robot enlightened them. "On the fifth of November 1605, Guy Fawkes and his Catholic followers plotted to blow up the Houses of Parliament to overturn the Protestant government. The plot was foiled, and on subsequent anniversaries Guy Fawkes' Night is celebrated with bonfire parties at which effigies of Guy Fawkes, commonly known as guys and similar in construction and appearance to scarecrows, are burned on bonfires. The traditional accompaniment of fireworks is less popular now for reasons of health and safety."

"Guy Fawkes, Marcia? Boy, these Brits sure choose weird names."

"They certainly do, Randy."

He changed up a gear as they sped through open country. "But why do they need so many? Isn't one Guy Fawkes enough for them?"

Marcia shuddered. "Burning even one is one too many for me. And at the vicar's house, too. He doesn't sound like a man of God. Let's head back to the safety of a city. The English countryside is way too dangerous."

But the danger had barely begun. Had Randy and Marcia remained after nightfall, they'd have found fifty-four guys about to be burned on the bonfire, with one real person concealed among them.

2 The Tangled Web

Now that it was October, and the bookshop's start-of-term sales had fallen away, the proprietor Hector Munro and I were busy setting up a Halloween window display to lure people back in. Hector told me Halloween was a big thing in Wendlebury Barrow, and I was looking forward to a bit of fun to liven up the shorter days of autumn. I'd only come to live there the previous June, when I inherited my Great Auntie May's cottage and landed a job as a sales assistant at Hector's House, the local bookshop. There was still so much for me to learn about this village that I'd started to think of as home.

As I sprayed fake cobwebs into the top left-hand corner of the bay window, Hector, standing on a small pair of steps, was suspending rubber spiders and bats on black thread from a series of display hooks permanently set into the ceiling. Plastic snakes writhed over spooky books artfully arranged beneath them.

Billy clattered through the shop door in time for his usual elevenses of tea and cake. "If you'd asked, I could have saved you the trouble and brought you some real cobwebs from home," he said. "And spiders."

Billy's loyalty to Hector's House was cemented not by a love of books, which he never bought, but by the illicit hooch that Hector brewed to slip into the tea of favoured guests. The cream of the bookshop, Hector liked to call it.

"No thanks, Billy, we're treating Halloween strictly as fiction," said Hector. "If we want to truly scare the village children, we'll send them round to yours. Pass me another bat, would you, Sophie?"

I had just set down my aerosol can and was rummaging in the props box when the shop door creaked open, and a new voice joined the conversation.

"You've omitted to dust the upper left-hand quadrant." The tall, lean stranger in a plain black suit addressed me, pointing to a fine cluster of cobwebs that I'd sprayed artistically into place. "A feather duster is the optimum weapon."

I smiled politely at what I presumed to be a feeble joke, until I realised from the stranger's grim expression that he was deadly serious.

"Trust me, my dear, I speak from experience. I've extinguished so many spiders in the vicarage this morning that I now count myself an arachnid expert."

His straggly white hair bore evidence of his morning's battle: a dead spider lay on his tonsure-like bald patch. If I were a spider, the stranger's steely grey eyes would have sent me scuttling for cover.

Hector climbed down from the steps and came to stand beside me as if to provide an informal welcoming committee. When he held out his hand for a handshake, the stranger gave it a disparaging look, as if it needed a good wash, and did not return the gesture.

"Good morning, sir. We haven't had the pleasure."

"Don't you believe it. I saw him kiss her the other day."

I could have murdered Billy. One impulsive kiss from Hector the previous week, when he congratulated me on winning a writing prize, was hardly a sin. To be honest, even if it was, I wouldn't have minded sinning again, never mind if it did upset the sanctimonious stranger. I bet he didn't get many kisses. That was probably why he was so sour.

With a diplomatic smile, Hector slipped his hands into the pockets of his jeans. "I mean, I don't think we've had the pleasure of seeing you in our bookshop before. Or have we?" He gazed at the stranger as if trying to place him. "I have a feeling we have met before, but I'm not sure where. You're not local, are you?"

The stranger looked smug. "My dear fellow, I am the most local vicar you will ever have in your emporium. I am indeed *your* vicar, the Reverend Philip Neep. I arrived last night as the new incumbent of the Parish of Wendlebury. This is therefore my first visit to your store." He stared at Hector for a moment, then quickly looked away.

Dropping the iced bun to which he'd helped himself from the tearoom counter, Billy almost ran over to join us. "Our new vicar? Welcome to Wendlebury, vicar. We wasn't expecting you till the end of November." He seized the vicar's right hand in his own, pumping it up and down in vigorous greeting.

The vicar peered down his long nose at Billy, who stood at least a head shorter than him, and was scruffy as ever in old buff cords, checked flannel shirt, and much patched tweed jacket.

"And you are?"

"Billy Thompson. I tend the churchyard and vicarage garden, with payment by the hour. I've been a member of the Friends of St Bride's these last twenty-three years and honorary treasurer for five."

The vicar tugged his ambushed hand free with a look of distaste and pulled a handkerchief from his top jacket pocket to wipe it clean. "Doubtless I shall see you again at their next meeting."

"Oh no, vicar, you're not on the Friends' committee. But we do occasionally liaise with the Parochial Church Council. That's your gang."

The vicar raised his eyebrows. "That will never do. I'm used to being closely involved with all the workings of my parish. After all, what is a vicar if not everyone's friend?" He turned his back on Billy to address Hector again. "My parishioners can be so thoughtful about not overtaxing me, but to serve my community is my reason for being."

Frowning, Billy returned to his table to take solace in the remainder of his iced bun. "What about serving God?" he muttered with his mouth full.

Abruptly, the vicar pushed past Hector and me and started browsing the bookshelves. He paused by the autobiography section. "Rather a lot of celebrities here, I see." He pulled out a thick hardback by a famous supermodel with as much

6

disdain as if it carried a social disease. Flicking through its pages, he lingered over the shiny photographs.

"Not someone I'd consider worthy of commemoration. I'd rather read about a more inspiring role model with a humbler public profile. They'd certainly write better. Not that anybody recognises great writing when they see it these days." He coughed, his lungs probably still dusty from his morning's labours. "Most celebrity autobiographies are ghostwritten, you know."

I tried to lighten the vicar's mood with a joke. "Then we'd better add them to our spooky window display."

Ignoring me, he shoved the book back onto the shelf, oblivious to the fact that his rough handling had ripped its dustjacket. Almost as an afterthought, he added, "And where is your spiritual section? I assume you have a wide selection of Bibles?"

Hector pointed to the bottom shelf in the furthest corner. "Faiths are down there, next to Philosophy, just along from Self-help."

"Faiths?" The vicar pronounced the final s as if it were a second superfluous syllable. He stooped to inspect the evidence. "Buddhism? Judaism? Druids? That's not what I asked for at all."

Hector, ever the diplomat, was trying hard to remain civil. I could tell he didn't like Mr Neep's rudeness to me or to Billy, even though Billy was frequently rude to everyone else. At least Billy had his heart in the right place. I wasn't sure Mr Neep had a heart at all.

"I stock what my customers are most likely to buy," Hector explained patiently.

The vicar swivelled round on his heel, looking like a headmaster about to chastise a schoolboy. "But, my dear fellow, if you don't stock a good range of Bibles, how can your clientele buy them? Equally the memoirs of some more deserving fellows?"

I could tell Hector's teeth were gritted beneath his tolerant smile. "My limited stock is carefully curated to meet the tastes of my customers. If someone wants to buy something that's not in stock, I place a special order for no extra charge. Such are the ways of the successful bookseller. But perhaps it would help us get to know each other better if you joined me for a pot of tea, vicar?"

"Moral high ground to you, young Hector," murmured Billy, sucking a stray bit of icing off his thumb.

Crossing to the tearoom, Hector pulled out a chair at the table furthest from Billy and gestured to the vicar to sit down. "I hope we'll see you here often."

Once the vicar had taken the proffered seat, I rushed over to serve him and Hector tea. The vicar looked dubiously at the cup and saucer as I set them before him. Our book-themed crockery is provided by the Literally Gifted company in return for us promoting its products in our shop, and I'd inadvertently given him the *Dracula* tea cup.

"I'm sorry, I think that cup's cracked," I said, although it wasn't. "I'll get another."

I swiftly replaced it with *Pride and Prejudice* to match Hector's *Persuasion*, and gave *Dracula* to Billy instead. As I filled the *Great Expectations* teapot, Hector tried to move the conversation on to safer ground.

"I'm so glad to see they have brought you here to fill the vacancy at last. We've been vicarless for months."

"Better than being knicker—"

Fortunately the vicar had his back to Billy, so didn't see me clasp my hand over the old boy's mouth to silence him. I don't usually assault our customers, and Billy took it in good spirit, seizing the opportunity to kiss my palm. I whisked my hand away as fast as I could, secretly glad that Billy was standing up to the vicar's rudeness.

While I gave my hands a very thorough wash behind the tearoom counter, Hector pressed on.

"I hope we'll have the opportunity to welcome your wife here soon, vicar. There are plenty of clubs and societies in the village that would be glad of her company. My assistant Sophie is a member of the Wendlebury Writers and the Show Committee. I'm sure she'd be happy to make introductions."

"Dead," said the vicar. "My wife is dead."

"I'm so sorry." Hector fell silent.

I wondered whether being widowed was what had made the vicar so judgmental about me and Hector. He must have been lonely.

Billy beckoned me back to his table. "Slip him some of Hector's special cream. That'll soften the old bugger up a bit."

I fetched the jug from the fridge.

"Would you like some cream in your tea, vicar? We do a very nice local cream for special guests. We like to support local producers."

"I take it black."

Daunted, I splashed a little into Hector's cup. He looked grateful.

"So, what do you do in this bookshop of yours?" The vicar asked as if it wasn't a bookshop at all, but a thinly veiled front for an opium den. I quickly set the cream jug down on Billy's table before the vicar could get a whiff of its contents.

Hector rattled off the description that I recognised from the shop's website. "We offer much more than books, stationery and greetings cards to the local community." He indicated the various display racks. "We provide a free meeting place for all ages and interests, such as the Wendlebury Writers and book groups. Our staff offer professional coaching in reading and writing for children who need extra help outside of the school day. We also lay on seasonal children's activities and themed events for adults, to promote a love of books and reading all year round." He pointed to the pile of free witch and ghost activity sheets on the play table in the corner. "We're very much involved with the life of the village school. I presume you will be too, vicar, given that it's a Church of England foundation school?"

"Yes, it will certainly be the school's priority to have me guide the spiritual growth of the children and the staff."

I wasn't sure that was how the school staff might see it. Although the school had been founded by the church, leaving a lasting connection between the two, I knew from the pages of the parish magazine that currently top of the staff's wish list was a new interactive whiteboard for the school hall followed by someone to repaint the hopscotch grids in the playground.

But the vicar had his own ideas. "I shall bring a wealth of new ideas and inspiration to the local educational establishment. "And on that note, I must ask you to remove all Halloween stock from your shop forthwith."

Hector took a deep breath.

"More tea, vicar?" I said brightly, stepping forward to raise the pot to buy Hector thinking time. I could see this was going to be a two-pot problem. Mr Neep put his hand over his cup to refuse a refill as Hector began to speak.

"I'm sorry, vicar, but that's quite impossible. As always at this time of year, we stock a wide range of Halloween books and activity materials." He waved his hand towards our boxes of decorations. "We always celebrate Halloween in this village, but it's all just a bit of fun. No real witchcraft here, ha ha. Besides, this is an independent bookshop. I make my own decisions about stock and policy. My shop, my rules. So we will continue to cater for our customers' interest in Halloween as usual."

The vicar shuffled back his chair, knocking the table hard enough to spill tea from the cups into the saucers. "Then I'm afraid I cannot conduct business with you, sir."

Hector looked taken aback. "Why ever not? Your predecessor was one of our best customers. Particularly keen on police procedurals, as I recall."

Neep slammed his hands down onto the table so hard that I feared he might break the china. Then he screwed up a paper serviette that he had not even used and threw it down. It might as well have been a gauntlet.

"Halloween is an ungodly festival which promotes Satanism. As a man of the church, I will not patronise premises that lionise the work of the devil. Good day to you."

He rose to his feet, stalked out of the shop, and slammed the door behind him, leaving Hector calmly sipping the rest of his tea.

Billy broke the ensuing silence. "He ain't no proper vicar, if you ask me. Why did old Reverend Murray have to go and retire? He was what I'd call a real man of the cloth. Someone with a bit of common courtesy and respect for his fellow parishioners. Used to buy me a bottle of Scotch every autumn, in return for clearing up his dead leaves."

Crossing over to the window, Billy picked out from our Halloween props box the ugliest, most misshapen fluffy spider he could find, and tied a black cotton thread around its middle. Then he pulled a black rubber band out of his sagging jacket pocket. Roughly he slipped the rubber band around the spider's neck. Taking a bottle of correction fluid from the shop counter, he dabbed a patch of white on the rubber band just beneath the spider's mouth, creating a passable impression of a clerical dog collar. Shakily, he clambered up the stepladder to suspend the spider from the hook in the centre of the shop window's ceiling.

"Let him put that in his organ pipe and smoke it," said Billy tersely, batting the spider to send it spinning in wild circles.

I expected Hector, always respectful of his customers, to leap up, remove the spider and rip off its makeshift clerical collar. Instead, he raised his teacup to Billy in a toast.

"Amen to that."

I had a feeling the new vicar's tenure would not end well.

3 The Wisdom of Joshua

Having never met the previous vicar, I was unsure how different Mr Neep was from the norm. The only evidence I had to go on so far was that the Reverend Murray had liked to ply Billy with Scotch and read books about criminals.

Not confident of objective information on the subject from either Billy or Hector, I decided to wait until after work to ask my next-door neighbour, Joshua. As the longest standing resident in the village, he, of all people, would be able to give me the low-down. He had never lived anywhere other than the cottage next to mine, where he'd been born eighty-six years before.

When I got home, I went through my small front room to the kitchen, dumped my coat and my handbag on the table as usual, filled the electric kettle and turned it on. As I did so, I spotted Joshua in his back garden, picking the last few runner beans from his immaculate vegetable plot. I unlocked the back door and strolled down the path to greet him, wrapping my arms about me for warmth. I wasn't sure he should have been out gardening in this weather.

He set down a wicker basket of impressively long, straight beans and put one hand to his back.

"Good evening, my dear," he said, although it was only just gone five. I've noticed mornings and evenings start earlier when you're old. "What can I do for you this fine autumn night?"

"I need to pick your brains," I began.

"Beans? I've just picked more than I can eat. I want to get them in before Jack Frost touches the vine. You're welcome to some if you like. My teeth can't take them this big and tough. I'm not sure why I still grow them. Force of habit, I suppose. Hard to change your ways after seventy years of doing something."

I admired the contents of his basket.

"Brains, not beans. I wanted to ask your advice about something."

"Over a pot of tea?" he said hopefully. Picking up his walking stick and the basket of beans, he followed me through the low wooden gate that he and Great Auntie May had installed between their gardens after his wife Edith had died. Joshua and May had been sweethearts until she had gone abroad to pursue her career as a travel writer, only resuming their relationship decades later, after he had been widowed.

Once indoors, he set the basket on my kitchen table and settled himself in his usual wheelback chair, leaning his stick against its arm. I'd only once taken tea in his house, which was when I'd spotted that he missed bits when washing up. After that, I'd engineered it so that he always came to mine, an arrangement he seemed to appreciate.

Although Joshua's mind was still razor sharp, it could sometimes wander off a bit. It seemed today it was still in the garden.

"Of course, the coming of the frost is not all bad. Although it takes the beans, it brings out the full flavour of the sloes for sloe gin. Take my advice, Sophie, never pick your sloes until after the first frost."

"I've still got some of Auntie May's sloe gin." I brandished a small bottle that I'd left on the windowsill to admire its luscious colour in the autumn sunshine. "There's quite a stock of it in the larder beside her home-made raspberry jam."

He raised his eyebrows in anticipation. "There won't be for long once the cold winter nights set in. May and I have had some very pleasant evenings over a glass of sloe gin."

I feared he might be about to tell me more than I needed to know, so I pressed on with my burning reason for inviting him in.

"It's about the new vicar, Mr Neep." I filled the teapot from the freshly-boiled kettle. "We had a visit from him today at Hector's House."

"He's here already? That's good news. I'm looking forward to becoming acquainted with him. The only member of the parish who has met him so far is Katherine Blake, chair of the PCC, the Parochial Church Council. That was just before she departed for her extended holiday in Australia five months ago, a day or two before you arrived in the village, Sophie. She told me she was very taken with him, and that's good enough for me. Besides, we've been without a vicar far too long – since just after Easter, when we lost dear May."

I filled the milk jug from the carton in the fridge and set out May's best bone china cups and saucers for us. Joshua preferred cups to mugs, as had Auntie May.

"Well, I'm not sure it is good news, Joshua. He struck me as the opposite of everything a vicar ought to be. Cold, bossy, humourless. I found him a bit scary, to be honest. And he had no sense of fun."

Joshua watched me pour his tea. "I don't believe a vicar's job description includes a sense of fun. It's a serious job, being a parish priest. Very responsible, and not for the faint-hearted."

I took the lid off the biscuit tin and offered him one of his favourite shortbread biscuits. "Even so, surely he shouldn't be interfering with local businesses? He just told us to take down our Halloween decorations and not to stock any Halloween books. That's not very kind, is it?"

Joshua looked unperturbed. "My dear, you can hardly expect a Church of England vicar to embrace Halloween. Plenty of good Christians would agree with him on that score, myself included. His focus will be on the church calendar. All Saints' Day on the first of November and All Souls' Day on the second." He glanced up at the calendar hanging from a nail above the kitchen table, displaying Japanese flower paintings, hung by my late great aunt before she died. "All Souls' Day is for remembering departed loved ones, not for dressing up as witches and wizards and playing tricks on each other. Besides, Halloween did start out as a religious festival. Hallow, as in 'hallowed be thy name'."

I frowned. I knew the Lord's Prayer off by heart, but I'd never noticed the hallowed connection before.

"Hector said the Reverend Murray never minded. Apparently he even went to the PTA Halloween Disco in fancy dress."

"Yes, as the Pope," said Joshua tersely. "Highly inappropriate. His wife went as Mother Teresa."

I suppressed a laugh. "Still, it's hardly the best way for Mr Neep to win over his new flock. If I had just arrived in the village, I'd be falling over myself to make new friends. I'd presume the best of people until I had proof to the contrary." I thought it better not to let on that when I'd moved here the previous June, I'd suspected Joshua of being a serial killer who had bumped off his late wife Edith and Great Auntie May and of having murderous intent towards me.

Joshua drained his cup, set it back neatly on its saucer and looked hopefully at the teapot. "I agree that he ought to get to know us properly before he criticises or tries to change our ways."

"Exactly. Especially in a nice, friendly place like Wendlebury Barrow."

He watched me splash the right amount of milk into his cup before I poured in more tea. I knew he subscribed to the 'milk in first' theory.

"My advice cuts both ways, my dear. Villagers should get to know the newcomer better before passing judgment."

Feeling like Sherlock Holmes slipping urchins a sixpence in return for streetwise intelligence (Hector had just given me *The Adventures of Sherlock Holmes* to read), I offered Joshua another biscuit.

"I'm glad we didn't have to wait any longer for him," Joshua continued after chewing a bite of shortbread for a very long time. "As far as I remember, he was meant to leave his previous parish at the end of November, and join us just in time for Advent." He brushed biscuit crumbs from his corduroy trousers. "I'm sure that's what Katherine said. No doubt on her return there'll be a letter from the Diocese on her doormat telling us of the change of plan. Or perhaps she has been sent one of those emailing messages that you young people like to use."

I swished the last drop of tea around my cup, wondering whether Mr Neep had been drummed out of his previous parish early so they could have a jolly good Halloween party in his absence. Not wanting Joshua to think me unkind, I didn't say that aloud.

Joshua smiled. "I'm just grateful that he's here. It can be hard to fill a vacancy in a small rural parish such as ours. That's why there's been no-one in post since before May's funeral. Poor May had to be buried by a stranger. We're lucky to have a vicar at all."

As I had been living and working in Germany when May died, I'd been unable to attend her funeral myself, but I remembered my father saying that it had been led by a vicar from another parish who didn't know her personally. I couldn't help feeling glad that Mr Neep hadn't arrived in time to officiate.

I could imagine him burying people who weren't quite dead.

"Thank you, Joshua, that explains at lot," I said. "But I can't promise I'll start going to St Bride's while he's in charge."

Joshua shook his head sadly. "That is the trouble with the shortage of vicars – not enough choice to match the priest to the parishioners. Put the wrong person in post, and a small congregation will wither further. But we must pull together as a village and make the best of it. As for me, I'm glad he's here in time to conduct the All Souls' Day service. I shall be there to say prayers for dear May as well as for my beloved Edith. Perhaps you might care to join me?"

I left the question unanswered, not wanting to go, but not wanting to say no, either.

"It's a positive celebration, my dear, not funereal at all," he added encouragingly, before pressing both hands down on the table in front of him to raise himself up from his chair. He picked up his walking stick. "And if you know of any youngsters planning to call at my door on Halloween, tell them from me that if they want free sweets, I'll expect them to sing for their supper."

He chuckled. I believed him, though I was sure he'd be generous with the subsequent treats.

Spookily, at that point there was a knock at my front door.

"You're popular this evening, young Sophie. I'll bid you goodnight. I'll leave you these beans in case you want to share them with your visitors. I shall lift the vine tomorrow as it's about finished now. Just pop the basket back over the wall when you're done with it."

Joshua moved slowly across the kitchen, catching hold of the sink as he passed it to steady himself. "Out with the old, in with the new!" He waved his stick in the air as he let himself out of the back door. I thought he'd make a great Old Father Time, come New Year's Eve – although I wouldn't want him to be mistaken for the Grim Reaper. After the events of the summer, when one of the Wendlebury Players had met her death during the Village Show, I hoped the village would be spared another visit from the Grim Reaper for a while.

My doorbell rang again. I hoped it wasn't the vicar making house calls.

4 The Play's the Thing

Who should it be but Ian and Mary, two of the remaining Wendlebury Players? I felt like I'd summoned them up with my thoughts of the Grim Reaper. There were only six of the Players left now.

Ian stepped forward. "Hello, Sophie, please may we come in?"

Never one to refuse a request from an executioner (Ian's role in the Players' Tudor tableau at the Show), I stood back to admit them into my small front room. I liked Ian, a tall, broad, jovial chap who was also the village lollipop man and school caretaker, and Mary had always been kind to me.

While Ian took the armchair, Mary sank down into the sagging couch, and I perched on the chair at May's small writing bureau.

"This is unexpected." I looked at them in turn, searching for clues as to the reason for this delegation. Had I offended them? "What can I do for you?"

"Don't sound so worried, Sophie," said Mary. "We've just come to tell you that we don't need to take you up on your kind offer after all."

"My kind offer?" Then I remembered that in my early zeal to fit into village life, and to seek revenge on my actor ex-boyfriend who had never let me get involved with his travelling theatre group, I had offered to write a play tailor-made for the Players' membership. I'd omitted to tell them that I'd never written a play before. Well, not one that had been performed, anyway. Damian had scorned all my scripts.

"We hope you don't mind," said Mary.

She couldn't have been more wrong. The weight of responsibility fell from my shoulders as quickly as it had landed there.

"No, not at all." Replying a little too hastily, I added for the sake of politeness, "I'm a bit disappointed, of course, but I'm glad you've found an alternative solution."

Mary looked relieved. "It was always tricky finding plays with a suitable cast list even before we lost poor Linda."

"Of course, we had to abandon *The Six Wives of Henry VIII* when we went down to five wives," said Ian.

"Besides, none of us want to wear those Tudor costumes, not when being trapped inside one of them hastened poor Linda's demise." Mary shuddered. Linda's body had been entirely concealed beneath her costume, which included a fake neck, as if post-execution, and she'd been wired into place on their show float to stop her falling off. No-one knew she was dead until the carnival parade was over. She'd been murdered in plain sight of all the crowds.

Ian looked glum. "Such a shame because it was a perfect match for our previous line-up."

Mary held up her hands in despair. "We tried to think of other plays that would work for us, but we've drawn a blank after going through every show with Five in the title. *Five Guys Named Mo* is no good because we're five girls, not five guys. *Five Children and It* would have been perfect, if only we were all just a little younger."

I was glad they'd learned their lesson from their last show, an ill-advised production of *The Sound of Music*, in which most of them featured as children.

"I wasn't confident the stage was strong enough to bear the weight of the Psammead's sandpit," said Ian, who is set designer, carpenter and engineer for each show. He's nothing if not versatile. "Which is a shame, as I wouldn't have minded being It. I've never had a title role before."

"For a while we thought the *Famous Five* might work," said Mary. "Until we remembered the fifth one is a dog. Ian was happy to play the inevitable villain, the smuggler or kidnapper or whatever the baddie turns out to be in each story, but none of us girls wanted to be the dog."

"How about *Five Brides for One Brother*?" I suggested.

Mary continued, "We've got the Village Hall booked for early December, three evening performances and a matinee, but we thought it would be unreasonable to expect you to write a play at such short notice. So we have been toying with the idea of a winter revue instead, with each of us doing a party piece of some sort."

That clearly got Ian's vote. "I'm going to play the Joel Gray role from *Cabaret*. It'll be ace."

"And I'm going to play Liza Minelli." Mary patted her round tummy. "I've started the diet for it already."

I'd watched the DVD of *Cabaret* about ten times when I was in Germany, and I loved it, but remembered it was an adults-only film. "I'm not sure the new vicar would approve," I said.

Mary leaned forward. "We've got a new vicar already? Have you met him? What's he like? The Reverend Murray and his wife loved our shows. They used to sing along to most of them. We always reserved seats in the front row for them so they could boost the chorus."

I nodded. "He's here, large as life, and was in Hector's House this morning, laying down the law about not leading the village children astray at Halloween."

Mary tutted. "Hector is very charming. You know all about that, don't you, Sophie? But he's hardly the Pied Piper of Hamelin."

I couldn't help but blush. I didn't think anyone else had noticed my crush on my boss. I was glad when Ian steered the conversation back on track.

"Besides, we like our Halloween celebrations. They're harmless enough."

"We don't want to fall out with the new vicar," said Mary. "But we've got to have a pre-Christmas show, or we'll lose our momentum, and that'll be the end of the Wendlebury Players."

Ian drew a finger across his throat. "So it looks like we'll have to think again about our choices of song."

Mary sighed. "Honestly, it would just be so much easier if we had a decent script, as usual."

Before I knew what I was saying, I found myself volunteering again.

"My offer to write a script for you is still on, if you'd like me to. Just tell me when you'd need the script by."

Mary delved into her handbag and pulled out a WI pocket diary. "Two Thursdays' time?"

"Oh good, no pressure, then." For two pins I'd have rescinded my offer, but seeing their anxious faces, I resolved not to let them down. After all, I counted the remaining Players as my friends, and I had made them a promise.

I held up my hand. "Don't worry, I'll come up with something by then. Just leave it with me."

I stood up, hoping they'd get the hint to leave. I needed all the time I could get between now and then to come up with a script from scratch. Then, feeling guilty for not inviting them to stay for a cup of tea, I darted out to the kitchen to grab Joshua's basket.

"Like some runner beans to take home with you?"

Mary smiled at me pityingly. "Sophie, haven't you learned yet? You can't give runner beans away in the country at this time of year. We're all sick of the sight of them by the end of the season. But I'll take them off your hands. It's kind of you to offer. You've

27

done very well to grow such big ones in the short time you've been here."

Once I'd ushered them out of the door, I lay down on the sofa to rack my brains as to what kind of play I might write to keep everyone happy – the Wendlebury Players, the audience, and our strange new vicar.

5 Solidarity Between Shops

After Ian and Mary left, I ended up abandoning my brain racking in favour of watching a feel-good movie, curled up on the sofa under a blanket with a ready-meal, before a hot bath and bed. Next morning, I awoke with a brilliant idea about where to find inspiration for my script. I've noticed your subconscious solves problems for you while you're asleep. I was glad it had come to my rescue again.

As I walked up to work through the crisp autumn sunshine, I tried not to dwell on my disappointment at having to watch yet another romcom on my own the night before. My relationship with Hector had not progressed beyond that tantalising first kiss, but I didn't want my unrequited affections to distract me from the task in hand for the Players.

I'd left home a few minutes early for once, to allow time to call in at the village shop to consult Carol about the Wendlebury Players' wardrobe, of which she was manager. As the bell above the door pinged to announce my arrival, Carol looked up mournfully from behind a mountain of runner beans which she was trying to arrange in a neat stack, Jenga style. A small heap of offcuts lay beside a pair of scissors she'd used to trim them to equal length to make the task more feasible. In the clear, cool morning light, the acid-green pile of fresh pods was almost fluorescent against the pyramid of shiny orange pumpkins behind them. The beans' familiar astringent fragrance was swamped by the smell of Pledge, which I suspected Carol had been using to give the pumpkins a good polish.

"Can I interest you in some nice locally-grown running beans?" she asked doubtfully. "Mary's just brought me even more."

I hoped that if Joshua came up to the shop, he wouldn't recognise his own produce. "No thanks, Carol, I'm not food shopping right now. I've just come to see you about wardrobe matters."

Carol pointed listlessly towards the back of the shop. "You'll find mothballs between menthol crystals and mouthwash."

"No, not my wardrobe, the Wendlebury Players' one." I set my handbag down on the counter. "You see, I've been asked to write them a play to replace their cancelled Henry VIII show, and I can't decide what it should be about. Given the short notice, I thought I'd take my inspiration from whatever costumes you've got already made up in the wardrobe."

"There's my lovely Tudor ones. I spent hours on those blessed frocks. Those muffs were a nightmare to iron, but the overall effect was beautiful. It would be a treat to see those on stage." It was true, except she meant ruffs, not muffs – snow-white pencil-pleated linen ones. "Apart from the outfits the police took away as evidence for the trial of Linda's murderer, of course."

I hesitated. "It might be a little insensitive to bring them out again so soon, especially as Linda's relatives might be in the audience."

Carol fiddled with the top layer of beans. "Then I'm not sure I can be of much help, Sophie. We've only got the costumes for the last couple of shows that we've done. We had to have a big clear-out last year, because some squirrels had nested in the costume cupboard over the winter and made a real mess." She wrinkled her nose at the memory. "We had to throw almost everything away and start again. The only other outfits I can offer are nuns or oversized children's outfits made of old chintz curtains."

I grimaced. "That is a bit limiting."

"Or you could borrow costumes from my Halloween rail."

I didn't know about her Halloween rail, having never been in the village at this time of year. "What's that?"

"I make costumes all year round ready for children – and adults – to buy for Halloween. All sorts, I've got. Disney princesses, superheroes, witches, wizards, dragons, goblets, elvers. I've been doing it for years. Until now."

"But why stop now?"

"That blessed new vicar, that's why. That Reverend Neep called in last night to tell me Halloween's cancelled. He doesn't want anyone to go trick-or-treating. But to look on the bright side, we're all welcome to join him in church a couple of days later for All Souls' Day." She gave a watery smile. "I usually go to that anyway, to remember my

dear departed mum and dad. But not in fancy dress."
Carol sighed. "I did try to tell him how nicely we do
Halloween in the village. No tricks, just treats, with
children going around in costume to entertain their
neighbours, wishing them 'Happy Halloween'. Not
everybody joins in, but those that do get right into
the spirit of it. Some of the grown-ups even dress up
themselves to hand out sweets to callers. We have a
good system. If you're happy for children to knock
on your door for sweets, you just leave a lighted
pumpkin lantern on your front wall. What's the
harm in that?"

I pursed my lips. "Halloween isn't cancelled,
Carol. It will still be Halloween on the thirty-first of
October. It's just that the vicar doesn't approve of
it. And there's the PTA Halloween Disco Saturday
week, on the twenty-ninth. People will still need
costumes for that." I was pinning my hopes on the
PTA Halloween Disco to move things along with
Hector. It had potential as our first date. "Besides,
the vicar has no power to stop us doing anything. I
think he's just throwing his weight about. He tried
to pull the same trick on Hector yesterday. When he
saw us decorating the window for Halloween, he
told us to take the whole lot down again and ditch
our seasonal stock. As you can imagine, Hector will
be doing no such thing."

Carol started picking hairs off a particularly thick
bean.

"Besides, it's your shop, Carol. He can't tell you
what to do. What's the problem?"

She kept her eyes downcast. "The thing is, Sophie
– and please don't say anything to anyone else about

this – but living out here at my age, I don't meet many eligible single men. And I hear the vicar's a widower. I don't want to get on the wrong side of him before he's been here five minutes. You never know, he might be my last chance of happiness."

I couldn't begin to fathom just how lonely Carol must be to consider hooking up with that prince of darkness. I reached out and stilled her fidgeting hands, covering them with my own.

"Don't say that. I had no idea you were looking for a partner. Believe me, there are better places to look, better men out there than Mr Neep. I'll help you find someone much more suitable, I promise. Stick to your guns, set up your Halloween rail and vicar be damned."

She looked up at me wide-eyed. "Sophie, you'll be struck down, damning a vicar." Deep in thought, she brought a piece of bean up to her mouth and chewed it contemplatively. "But you're right. I don't want to disappoint anybody, and I can't afford not to sell my Halloween costumes. It wouldn't matter as much if I could make the money up by selling fireworks for Guy Fawkes' Night the following week, but I can't get a licence. I haven't got a lockable cupboard to store them in, and there's no room between the false eyelashes and the flour for them. Anyway, most people don't go in for fireworks at home any more. They're too worried about their children getting hurt. If they want to see a firework display, they go down to the big council one at Slate Green, where no-one can get anywhere near the bonfire or the fireworks."

"Well, there you go, decision made."

Carol nodded sadly. "Yes, you're right, Sophie. I just hope it doesn't put the vicar off me for ever."

Disappointed that I had not convinced her that Mr Neep wasn't her only romantic hope, I wondered who else I might be able to rustle up for her. I decided to put that plan on hold till I'd resolved my playwriting crisis. I'd get the play out of the way first and make Carol's love life my special project after that. How wonderful it would be if I could play matchmaker in time for Valentine's Day, or even Christmas.

At that moment, the church clock struck nine, making me realise that my immediate priority should be to get to work. I grabbed my handbag. "Excuse me, Carol, I must get on, or Hector will be after me."

"I wish Hector was after me," I heard her say as I dashed out of the door into the cold morning air.

6 Printer's Devil

By the time I arrived, breathless, at Hector's House, the bookshop was well and truly open. A couple of middle-aged tourists were sitting at one of the tearoom tables, poring over an Ordnance Survey map of the Cotswolds.

"We didn't get you up, did we?" asked Hector, quietly enough for only me to hear, as I dashed in, shrugged my coat off and unwound my long knitted scarf from around my neck. I slung my handbag behind the shop counter, and Hector stepped neatly aside to prevent it hitting his ankles. He pretended to fix me with a stern look, but I spotted the twinkle in his eye. "Still, it's good to see you've had plenty of beauty sleep."

"Hector, you are such a sexist sometimes." I hoped he could not tell that his comment had made my morning.

Once I'd served the tourists morning coffee and advised them on the best route to drive from Wendlebury to Cheltenham, I returned to the shop counter to fill Hector in on the conversation I'd just had with Carol about Halloween. I didn't mention her secret plan to marry the vicar, but inwardly pledged to be on the lookout in the bookshop to find her someone more suitable. Except Hector.

Then the business of the morning took over.

When Billy arrived for his elevenses, Hector put Frank Sinatra's "One More for the Road" on the sound system to welcome him, and I added Billy to my list of exceptions for Carol.

"Do you dress up on Halloween, Billy?" I asked, placing a pot of tea on the table in front of him. I was hoping the occasion might cause Hector to get out the Greek toga he'd worn as Homer on the Wendlebury Writers' carnival float.

"Yes, this year I'm going to dress up as a bloody vicar. That'll teach 'im. How about you, girlie? Fancy being my tart?"

Hector, sitting behind the till, spluttered into his morning coffee, but quickly recovered. "Oh, I see. Tarts and vicars. Very funny, Billy. No, Sophie will be dressing as something much more suitable." That was news to me. "A character from a children's book, as part of a programme of Hector's House Halloween events on the day itself, Monday the thirty-first of October."

Billy fixed Hector with narrowed eyes. "There's tarts in *Alice in Wonderland*."

"I was thinking more of something like *The Worst Witch*," said Hector.

"Can't I be a competent one instead?" I asked.

Hector considered. "All right then, how about the Narnia witch? I'll be the Lion, you can be the Witch, and Billy can be the Wardrobe."

I liked that idea. I was fond of Turkish Delight, and Hector did have the sinewy strength of a lion.

Lifting heavy book boxes all day can do things to a man.

Billy was not amused. "I think we should all be vicars."

"What, you mean like the 'I'm Spartacus' scene in the Kirk Douglas film?" Hector laughed. "'I'm the vicar.' 'No, I'm the vicar.' 'No, I'm the vicar.'"

I made a mental note to Google "Kirk Douglas Spartacus quotes" when Hector wasn't looking.

"That's all very well, so long as no-one decides that Halloween is the perfect night to bump off Mr Neep," said Billy, tipping more cream into his cup. "Which it would be, because everyone would just blame the devil. I don't want to go getting myself killed for the sake of a joke."

Hector came across to remove the cream jug from Billy's table and put it back in the fridge. He didn't completely abdicate responsibility for Billy's alcohol consumption for the sake of the shop's profits. "If Mr Neep was bumped off, you'd be number one suspect."

Billy pointed to the spidery Mr Neep still suspended in the shop window. "I think that honour lies with you, young Hector."

Billy had a point. Hector didn't usually risk upsetting customers, never mind displaying effigies of them in his shop window. The fact that Billy had made the effigy did not excuse him.

Hector went quiet, leaving Billy to continue.

"Actually, I think I'll go as God. Pull rank, like. That'll put the frighteners on the old bugger. I've got the beard for it. You told me so yourself, Hector Munro." He got up to retrieve the cream jug. "And

37

if you don't show a little more appreciation, Father Christmas will be on strike this season."

Incredulous, I swung round to face Hector. "You've got Billy playing Father Christmas? *Billy?*"

"Oh, it's all right." Hector waved my concerns aside. "I always tell the children he's not allowed to say anything, and that he just comes to listen to what they ask for."

I watched Billy drain the cream jug into his tea. "You'd better tell him not to breathe on them either."

Once Billy had wended his way home, or rather to The Bluebird for lunch, I gave the tearoom a quick clean. Then I took the opportunity while the shop was empty, which it rarely was, to buttonhole Hector for a private conversation that I needed to have soon or I'd go mad.

I began slowly and cautiously. "Hector." So far, so good.

"Hmmm?" He didn't look up from his computer screen, no doubt stuck in to typing his latest romantic novel. He moonlighted under the pen-name Hermione Minty to help fund the upkeep of the shop, and I was the only one in the village who knew his secret.

"Hector, you know the other day?"

"Any particular other day?" His voice was mild. "There have been a few." A staccato flurry of keyboard strokes suggested he was saving and printing his latest chapter. I'd picked a good moment to pin him down, yet I had to wonder at his deliberately being so obtuse.

"You know which day." I swallowed, trying to muster my courage. I could have done with a quick swig of the bookshop's cream. "The day you told me I'd won those writing prizes. The day you kissed me."

I'd won first prize in the Village Show's new writing competition for penning 250 words about Auntie May's garden, and a week at a writers' retreat in a national contest for which Hector had entered me without my knowledge.

He stood up and looked directly at me, his green eyes apologetic beneath his dark curls.

"Well, the thing is, I thought at the time that it meant you liked me."

"It did. I mean, I do."

He looked at his nails awkwardly.

"No, I don't mean just liking me. I mean, as in fancying me, or wanting to go out with me. But as nothing like that has happened since, I'm now wondering whether I took it the wrong way. I must have misconstrued it." I hesitated, hoping he'd interrupt to cut short my misery. Silence. "Ah. I see now it was your way of congratulating me. But I had to ask, just to be sure."

Hector rubbed at a non-existent mark on his thumbnail as I rambled on.

"You were just being kind. I apologise for any confusion. My fault entirely."

There was another moment of silence, then, "Sophie." That one word, spoken huskily with a slight tremor in his voice, was enough to make my spirits do a swift about-turn. "Sophie, that's not how it is at all. I'm sorry, I'm just bad at reading relationships."

I tried to alleviate his obvious embarrassment with a joke. "Bad at reading relationships? That's an unfortunate trait in a bookseller. Anyway, you are very good at reading people. Look at how you know which music to play to keep each customer happy."

He smiled, proud of his party trick. Then his expression became more serious. He stared at the floor. "I thought when I kissed you I'd overstepped the mark. After all, I am your employer. I was worried that I was taking advantage, harassing you with unwanted attentions. Billy did say something along those lines at the time."

"Sexy harassment" was how Billy had put it when he'd walked in to the shop and caught us in the act.

"Ha! Since when did you take etiquette advice from Billy?"

Hector looked sheepish. "I know. But even so, I thought I'd offended you and didn't know how to make amends."

"Offended? Me? If that was offensive, I'm Virginia Woolf!"

I wished I hadn't been so transparent. Retaining a little mystery never does a girl any harm.

Hector chuckled. "Well, I always did love a bluestocking." He inhaled sharply as he realised he'd said the L word. "Maybe I should reiterate."

He leaned towards me over the counter, grasped my right hand, raised it to his lips and kissed it. His half-apologetic smile sought permission to proceed. With the edge of the counter digging uncomfortably into my waist, I clasped my hands behind his neck and pulled him towards me. He kissed me gently at first, as if still half-afraid I might pull back and slap his face. Then he relaxed, and started kissing me with such passion that I realised he'd been bottling it up ever since the day of our first embrace. As had I.

Always leave them wanting more, I told myself, wishing to keep the upper hand.

"Oh, Hector!" I squealed, coming up for air. When he released me, I darted behind the counter and threw myself into his open arms. I lay my head contentedly on his shoulder, for which he was the perfect height, and he stroked my hair. If I was a kitten, I'd have purred. Recognising the scent of his shower gel, tea tree and mint, I shivered with pleasure as I pictured him applying it in the shower earlier that morning. Minty by name…

"Oh no," he said suddenly, pushing me away. Would this man never make up his mind?

Then the shop door creaked loudly, indicating the arrival of a customer.

Hector told me afterwards what he'd seen the minute he'd opened his eyes. I was gratified to know that his eyes had been closed. Mr Neep was standing outside the shop, gawping open-mouthed. But his expression of horror was fixed not on the window display, now jam-packed with Halloween books and accessories, nor the clerical spider suspended above it, but on the sight of Hector and me locked in an embrace.

"Mr House! What in heaven's name do you think you are doing?" The vicar charged up to the counter. "Taking advantage of this poor child." His low voice seemed more threatening than if he'd shouted his accusations.

I leapt to Hector's defence. "I'm twenty-five! And I have absolutely no objections to Mr Munro's behaviour!"

Mr Neep looked only at Hector. Immediately, I regretted my choice of words, which made it sound as if Hector and I weren't even on first-name terms.

"If that is how you treat your staff, I shall have to insist the village school buys its books from an alternative emporium, for the moral safety of its young charges."

Then he strutted back out into the High Street, slamming the shop door closed behind him. As he marched off in the direction of the vicarage, he was muttering to himself and shaking his head like a madman.

Startled now on two counts, I staggered across to the tearoom and sat down heavily on the nearest chair. Hector remained where he was, gazing after the retreating figure. "Is it me, or does that man sound like he belongs to a different age?"

"Perhaps he's not the real new vicar at all, but one that's just arrived here from the Victorian era in a time machine."

"That would certainly explain his prim attitude. But there is something strangely familiar about him. I can't think where I would have met him before. Maybe he was the college chaplain when I was at university, someone with whom I had few dealings. Either that or he did something so bad to me in my past that I've subconsciously repressed the memory."

Shaking his mane of dark curls, Hector stood up and stretched, king of the bookshop once more. "Still, we'd better make sure he's not really going to scupper our relationship with the school. It's our single biggest customer. I'd like to think the school staff are too smart to listen to his nonsense, but they do have to keep on the right side of him, because of the school's historic connection with the church. He'll automatically be a governor because of his position as parish priest." He thought for a moment. "Do you think you could make some discreet enquiries with Ella Berry to see how they're getting on with him? It might seem better coming from you than from me."

"Sure. I'll see if she's up for a drink after work. I won't say anything about you. I'll just suss out what they think of him."

"Thank you, Sophie. And then, maybe—" He hesitated. "How about on Guy Fawkes' Night, we go out for a meal together, then hit the council fireworks display in Slate Green?"

Suddenly I completely forgot about the vicar. I could hardly believe my good fortune. I sensed it had cost Hector a lot of effort to ask me out, and although I didn't know why, it was not an offer I was going to refuse. I just wished we didn't have so long to wait. Fireworks Night was still a couple of weeks away.

I tried to think of a better setting than the village pub for a romantic first date.

"How about that new Chinese in Slate Green?"

Hector looked relieved. "Excellent idea, Sophie. There are some things I'd like to tell you without being overheard by people in Wendlebury."

My heart dropped like a stone down a well. Why was he so keen to be somewhere we might not be recognised? Perhaps he had another girlfriend in the village that I wasn't meant to know about. Maybe Neep was hiding some dark secret from Hector's past, and Hector wanted to get in with his confession before Neep told me. A vicar would of course be a better judge of character than me. Perhaps I had made an awful mistake about Hector, and given the chance, the vicar might prove to be my saviour.

Or did Hector just want to keep up his pretence to Carol that he was gay and therefore unavailable to her? If that was the case, it might help if he knew what Carol had confessed to me that morning.

"Carol's set her sights on Mr Neep, by the way. But don't tell her I told you."

"Set her sights? What, like with a crossbow? I bet she's not the first to do that."

"No, silly, I mean romantically. Poor Carol, she's so lonely, and she doesn't meet many unattached men in the village. It's not surprising that she sees him as an opportunity."

Hector groaned. "She must want her head examined. That man…"

He stared off into space, and our conversation fizzled out into awkward silence.

7 Away in a Nativity Play

When I texted Ella to see if she wanted to meet at The Bluebird that evening to compare notes about the new vicar, she was keen enough. From her reply, I sensed she was not about to found a fan club for him.

When I arrived, she was already sitting in our favourite quiet booth by the door with two glasses of wine lined up ready – a large house white for me and a red for her, and a packet of kettle chips split open for us to share. The minute I'd shed my warm winter coat and sat down on the bench seat opposite her, I could tell she had had a bad day.

"Go on, then, spill the beans."

She closed her eyes and sighed. "Please, don't mention beans, I'm sick to death of beans. We've had them every day for weeks with school dinners. I'll be glad when the first frosts come and kill off the vines."

"No, not runner beans. Whatever beans are making you look so miserable."

Ella took a long swig of her drink, then wrapped her hands around the glass for comfort.

"It's this new vicar."

She looked at me to appraise what I'd made of him before voicing her own opinion.

"Don't worry, he's not exactly my new best friend."

She smiled weakly. "Nor mine." Then she thumped her hands decisively on the table. "Honestly, you'd think he owned the school. Before he had even met the staff and had a proper tour, he started laying into me about our policies. Our disgraceful policies, to be precise. He doesn't think we should have the internet in school because it's full of filth and corruption."

"Well, that speaks volumes about what he gets up to on his computer."

"Then he thinks we should have a half-hour religious service in school every single day. I don't know how he thinks we'd fit that in. We have trouble squeezing in the curriculum as it is. It's not as if we never have religious assemblies. We do them for Christmas and Easter, and Eid and Diwali, even though we've no Muslims or Hindus on the roll." She paused for another sip of wine. "Our weekly Friday Celebration Service is lovely. Although it isn't overtly religious, it's always full of love, tolerance and human kindness – qualities which apply to all faiths worth having. I hope that if the vicar comes to one of those, he'll cut us some slack about daily assemblies, but he hasn't been here long enough to attend one yet."

"Have you invited him to this Friday's?"

"Yes, of course, although I'm half hoping he refuses to come, after how rude he was to me this morning."

I stared into my glass. "Surely he should be putting his objections to the Head and the Board of Governors, rather than having a go at you, Ella? I mean, I know your role as Business Manager is an important one, but you're not responsible for making the school policies, only for implementing them."

Ella set her glass down on a beer mat. "Damn right, Sophie. I get the impression he's just a bully. I'm hoping the Head and the Governors will put him straight."

I nodded. "I think so too. He was really trying it on in the bookshop this morning. He told Hector he's going to ban the school from ordering books at Hector's House if we don't remove our Halloween stock."

"For goodness' sake, he's meant to be a vicar, not a dictator." Ella snapped a kettle chip in half. "You can tell Hector not to worry. We won't take our custom elsewhere. School policy is to support local businesses so that they'll support us too. Besides, we'd never get as big a discount or as local a service from any other bookshop." She paused for a moment to eat the fragments of kettle chip. "To be honest, I can understand the vicar saying he doesn't like trick-or-treating. Not everyone wants a string of sugar-fuelled monsters banging on their front door all evening. Some of our teachers don't like it either, but he has no right to stop children doing it at all. That's for the parents to decide."

I shrugged. "Oh well, it'll be Christmas before we know it. That should pacify him."

"You'd think so, but no. He's also declared war on our plans for Christmas."

"But that's a church festival. How can he object?"

"I'll tell you over our second glass of wine." Ella drained her glass, and I took our empties to the bar, wondering as I waited for Donald to serve me what sort of vicar could disapprove of Christmas. By now nothing would surprise me about Mr Neep.

I returned with full glasses and a packet of salted mixed nuts.

"So what's wrong with the school's plans for Christmas, according to Neep?"

"Everything, apparently. But his main objection is that we always do a pantomime rather than a nativity play. A pantomime works well on so many levels." She counted the advantages on her fingers. "It saves us taking the kids to see a pantomime in a theatre. It gives them more scope to show off their dramatic and musical skills. And it's intentionally funny, unlike most nativity plays I've ever seen. They only make the audience laugh when they're not supposed to. Also, there are more decent parts in pantomimes, and it's easier to add in extra characters to give all the children something to say. Plus none of the girls cry because they haven't been picked to play Mary. Nor do the ones who get a speaking part get inflated ideas of their own importance."

She paused to lick stray grains of salt off her fingertip. "It also suits the parents' religious convictions, in that most of them don't have any. More parents will come to see a pantomime than a nativity play. Some of them are the sort of middle-class smart-arses who put 'Jedi' in the Census form when asked to state their religion, but most of them just aren't bothered. Those that are actively religious take care of their faith needs outside school. I explained all that to Mr Neep, but, oh no, he still says we have to do a nativity play, come what may. It'll be Bedlam."

"I think you mean Bethlehem, young miss." Billy appeared from nowhere to inspect what we were eating. "We always did nativity plays in my day at the village school, and it didn't do me no harm." Helping himself to a fistful of our nuts, he strolled off towards the bar, scratching his bottom with his free hand.

"I rest my case," said Ella.

I pitied the children whose innocent pleasures the vicar seemed bent on destroying. "Well, maybe you can do a cross between the two. Add a new and different angle that makes a nativity play more fun for them than a pantomime."

"How do you mean?"

I rummaged through the nuts to find an almond. "I've just had a brilliant idea. We can solve two village problems in one fell swoop. The Wendlebury Players need a new play script, and they've asked me to write one to suit their cast." I leaned in to speak confidentially. "Frankly, I've been stumped as to how to handle it. But your dilemma has given me a brainwave: we can combine the two projects. The Players can work together with the children, running weekend workshops for rehearsals so the play needn't eat into your school day, and they can give the kids some extra-curricular drama coaching. They'll all enjoy that. The Players will also help you

49

put on the play in the Village Hall. It would be positively educational."

Ella smiled for the first time that evening. "They'll love that. When they do the panto in the school hall, we have to make a temporary stage out of wooden blocks. There's always at least one child who falls off it or slips down between the cracks at some point. It will be great to be able to use the Village Hall with its proper stage." She thought for a moment. "But who will play which character? Like I said, we don't want the kids squabbling over the handful of key parts."

"I'll write the speaking parts for the adults, and it will be super cute if all the children play animals or angels. Ian will obviously have to be Joseph, and the five women can play the other key roles – Mary, the Three Wise Men, and the chief shepherd. Why don't we ask the teachers to join in too? The Head can be the Angel Gabriel, you can be the Innkeeper, and the rest of the staff can be shepherds."

Ella laughed and clapped her hands. "Typecasting or what? I could say, 'No room at the inn, but we have got a couple of spaces in Years 2 and 5.' That's brilliant, Sophie. It'll tick the box for community cohesion too."

I had to ask her to explain what that meant.

"The school's obliged to collaborate with the local community as much as it can. This will provide an ideal opportunity for the school and the community to work together. Do you really think you will be able to write an appropriate script in time?"

I waved my hand dismissively, with the confidence that comes after two glasses of wine. "Easy-peasy. I mean, it's not as if I don't know the story already, or the characters. All I need to do is to sell the idea to the Wendlebury Players and get Carol to make about a hundred new costumes."

"I'm sure I can convince the Head and the staff, not least because it'll mean a lot less work for them than the usual panto. Sophie, you are a gem!" She raised her arms in a cheer, and we did a quick two-woman Mexican wave.

Our celebrations were cut short by the pub door being flung wide open. Making as dramatic an entrance as a gunslinger in a Wild West saloon, Mr Neep, clad in his usual black, stood glowering in the doorway. Dirty brown dead leaves blew in from behind him to scatter about his feet.

8 Gunfight at The Bluebird

If we'd been in Hector's House, Hector by now would have been playing the theme music from *The Good, The Bad and the Ugly*, but here in the pub Mr Neep's entry was met with curious silence. The vicar stood in the doorway, slowly surveying the room as if wondering on whom to draw his gun.

Donald, the publican, was first to speak. "Ah, Mr Neep, welcome to The Bluebird." Like Carol and Hector, he was keen to keep on good terms with anyone who might be a source of potential business. Under the Reverend Murray's direction, The Bluebird had been a regular venue for wakes and wedding receptions, and Donald wasn't about to risk losing that income stream.

The vicar approached Donald to reply, but stopped a foot distant from the bar, as if fearful it might be infectious.

"Can I offer you a glass of sherry on the house, vicar?" Donald filled a large schooner and set it on the counter for him. "The Reverend Murray was always very fond of Harvey's Bristol Cream. He said drinking sherry was just one of many ways of worshipping God."

"A true man of the cloth is temperate in his ways," said the vicar.

Ella winked at me. "Not our Reverend Murray."

Turning his back on Donald, Mr Neep left the sherry glass untouched.

"Well, what did you come in here for, then?" called Billy from his game of dominoes in the far corner. Laughter rippled around the pub. The vicar swung round to skewer Billy with a look.

"I might ask you the same thing. And indeed, I might ask that question of all of you. Don't you have families at home that you're neglecting, domestic duties to attend to, instead of loitering mid-week indulging your addictions?"

"I'm just popping outside for a ciggie," said one of Billy's dominoes companions. He produced a battered pack of twenty from his shirt pocket and exited via the side door to the smoking area. Two more players followed. Billy stayed behind, settling back in his chair as if anticipating some worthwhile entertainment.

Donald, who never usually drank alcohol during opening hours, was pouring himself a Scotch. He forced a smile in Neep's direction. "I could do with you when it comes to closing time."

Ella's snigger set me off giggling, which unfortunately attracted the vicar's attention to our secluded booth. He hadn't noticed us when he arrived, but now stalked across and stood staring accusingly at our glasses of wine. I was glad I'd returned the empties when I'd ordered our second glass.

"I might have known I'd find you here every night," he said coldly, entirely without foundation. Ella and I seldom meet at the pub more than twice a week, and he'd never been there before in his life to catch us.

Ella nudged me under the table with the toe of her shoe, while raising her glass in a toast to Mr Neep. "It's only Ribena, sir." I sometimes think she spends too long associating with the school's naughtiest children, always her favourites.

I followed suit. "Apple juice," I said solemnly, before draining my glass to hide the evidence. Mr Neep seemed to be teetering on the brink of sniffing our breath for evidence, but I suspect his fear of germs held him back.

Without a word, he stalked back to the bar, turned to face away from Donald and held up his hand for silence. For a moment I thought he was going to launch into a sermon. Instead, we just got a trailer.

"The reason for my presence in this bar—" he practically spat out the word "—is to reach as many locals as possible in one place. Given that I have arrived too late to list any church services in this month's parish magazine—" here he flashed an accusing look at its editor, Ella, as if his poor timing was her fault "—I invite you to join me for Morning Prayer at eight o'clock this Sunday. The service will include my first sermon in this parish. The topic will be abstinence." He turned suddenly to glare at Ella and me. "Abstinence of all kinds."

Billy was undaunted. "Abstinence? That's that green French drink that makes you go blind, isn't it?" There was raucous laughter from his corner of the room.

The vicar ignored the jibe, or perhaps he didn't understand it. "There will also be an All Souls' service on the morning of the second of November. In the meantime, I suggest you spend the rest of the evening in the bosom of your family, where you belong."

"There ain't no bosoms in my house, vicar." That was Billy again, of course. "Though it's not for want of trying."

At that, Mr Neep left as abruptly as he'd entered. As the door slammed shut behind him, an indignant chorus of "Ooo-ooo-oooh!" went around the room.

"Don't you worry, young Donald," Billy called out, raising his glass of stout. "The vicar will have to work harder than that to make us give up the demon drink."

As Ella and I left at closing time, Donald told us his takings had doubled that evening, as everyone pledged their support to The Bluebird in kind. It seemed Mr Neep was making enemies wherever he went in Wendlebury.

9 Fancy Dress

I don't usually bother with Halloween, but Mr Neep's ruling made me keen to celebrate it this year as much as possible. I couldn't wait to call in at the village shop on the way to work next day to see what Halloween costumes Hector and I might hire to wear in the bookshop on the day itself.

"How about a nice pair of zombies?" said Carol. "I've got plenty of grisly face-paint to match."

I didn't like to explain that I wanted something more alluring.

"Or an undead bride and groom?"

That would have seemed a little forward when we'd not even had our first date. "Hector said it shouldn't be scary. Do you have anything to do with children's fairy stories?"

"Little Red Riding Hood and the Big Bad Wolf?"

"The wolf might frighten the little ones. And their grandmothers."

"I've got it! Beauty and the Beast!"

She flicked through the clothes rack and pulled out a shiny yellow nylon ballgown, weighed down by flounces from top to bottom. I held it against myself over my coat. It hung beautifully.

"Thanks, Carol, you're too kind. Though I'm not sure how Hector will take to the idea."

"I don't know, I think men probably like to be thought of as a bit of a beast." She giggled. "Even Hector."

From a nearby box full of masks and headdresses, she pulled out a lion's head with a magnificent mane and a noble expression. Her skill with a needle was truly remarkable.

"That's amazing, Carol. Do you make all these outfits from scratch every year?"

"Oh no, some people bring them back when they're done, so I can sell them again next year. You know what they're like about recycling round here."

The kind villagers probably did this to bolster Carol's meagre profits. I couldn't see that happening in Tesco.

Carol lovingly folded the two costumes, slipped them carefully into separate carrier bags, and handed them to me.

"Shall I put them on the Hector's House account, as you're wearing them for work?"

I nodded. "Perfect. Now all I have to do is break it to Hector he's going to be a beast."

"Gosh," said Carol wistfully, at which point I thought it best to take my leave.

As I entered the shop, Hector pressed "play" on his music app to greet me with "Hello, Dolly". Just right: not too serious at this early stage in our relationship, but chosen carefully and with affection.

"I've got our costumes." I held up the two bulging carrier bags. "I love my frock. I hope you'll like yours."

"My frock? We're not going to be Cinderella's Ugly Sisters, are we?"

I pulled a face as if I was offended. "No, but you do get to wear a frock-coat. It's very dapper."

Hector looked relieved. "Good. I wouldn't want to scare you away."

Once I'd left the bags in the store-room and started setting up for the post-school-run morning coffees, I decided it was time to drop a subtle hint that he might invite me to the PTA Halloween Disco.

"Tell me about the PTA Halloween Disco, then." I lifted the day's delivery of Eat My Words cakes out of their boxes and arranged them on the pressed glass cake stands. "Is it only for children or do adults go too?"

"All ages are welcome, whether or not they've got kids. It starts at 7.30pm, and it goes on till midnight, though the families with small children generally leave earlier."

"What's the music like? Is it children's party songs or a proper disco?"

"It gets more grown-up as the evening goes by, so the little ones have some they recognise, with lots of actions to join in with. It's more 'Macarena' than minuets, I'm afraid. I hope you weren't anticipating some sedate Jane Austen style salon."

I smiled. "No, that's the last thing I'd be expecting in Wendlebury. Although that would be a better match for our costumes."

59

"They usually throw in a few slow numbers around midnight." He gave me a knowing look. "So I hope you're not planning to turn into a pumpkin on me."

I felt a rush of warmth run through me. He was already assuming we'd be going there together.

After the mums and toddlers had gone, I brought out our costumes from the stockroom and produced them with a flourish from their bags – first mine, then Hector's. I held the ballgown up against me, and gave a little twirl to demonstrate how it would flare out while I was dancing.

"Lovely," said Hector.

Gratified, I handed him his azure frock coat and he slipped off his fleece to try it on over his t-shirt.

"It's a good fit." He stretched out his arms to demonstrate. "I've just realised I forgot to tell you my size. You guessed well."

"No, Carol did." She must have spent enough time gazing longingly at him to make an accurate assessment.

I reached in the bag to pull out navy velveteen trousers and a lace-fronted shirt, which he wasn't quite so keen on. When I produced the lion's head (it was a very capacious bag), Hector let out a cry of alarm.

"A severed head? What am I meant to be, a big game hunter on a night out?"

"No, silly, we're Beauty and the Beast. Like the fairy tale. You said you wanted a storybook-related theme, and that one's perfect."

"Can't I be Beauty?"

"No, you're definitely more of a Beast," I laughed as the shop door creaked open.

"You bring out the beast in me too, girlie," said Billy, sidling up to slip his arm round my waist. I wriggled out of his grasp and moved swiftly away.

"Will you be going to the PTA Halloween Disco, Billy?" Somehow I couldn't picture him on the dance floor. Or at least, I didn't want to.

"I might wander up once I've wet my whistle at The Bluebird with their Halloween guest beers. Pale as a Ghost Ale, Evil Critter Bitter, and all that. But you'll have to wait and see what I'll be wearing. I'm saving it as a surprise."

"Just coming as you are will be enough, Billy." Hector winked at me. "The undead, unadorned."

"I'm in my seventy-seventh year," said Billy proudly. "And I've every intention of living to be a hundred."

Reprobate as he was, I'd grown fond enough of Billy to wish he might achieve his ambition. I hoped the special cream in his tea might act as a preservative rather than hasten his end.

10 Frightening Writers

I'd been so carried away with the plans for Halloween that I'd almost forgotten about the Wendlebury Barrow Big Read. This was an event organised in the Village Hall by the Wendlebury Writers a few weeks into every new school term. Each member would read to the audience something they'd written since the last one.

I'd had a sudden panic when first hearing about this venture, having nothing in my ragbag of scribbles that would withstand a public airing. Fortunately Dinah, the Chair of the Writers' Group, unwittingly came to my rescue by suggesting that this time we should each read a passage by the author we'd posed as on our Village Show float. Although that got me off one hook, it hung me from another, because I'd never read a word by Virginia Woolf. I'd only chosen her as my literary hero for the float to try to impress Hector and my new writer friends.

Tuesday evening, therefore, found me in my front room poring over May's copies of Virginia Woolf's books. To my surprise, I found myself mesmerised by her writing, staying up into the early hours to finish reading *Mrs Dalloway*. Having been feeling a fraud, I turned up to the Big Read event feeling validated, like someone who'd just got religion.

As a surprise for the audience, we'd be wearing our carnival costumes. I was looking forward to wearing Auntie May's drop-waisted silk dress again, although this time with a thermal vest underneath for warmth. I'd also once more be donning my kitten-heeled shoes and putting my usually loose long hair up in a soft bun at the nape of my neck.

The point of the Big Read wasn't just for the Wendlebury Writers to show off their work – or, in this case, someone else's work. It also involved other villagers, who were welcome to bring pieces to read as well as to provide an audience. The group usually gained one or two new members this way each term.

We advertised the event in the October parish magazine and put notices up in the village shop, on the telegraph poles throughout the village (standard practice, it seemed, to spread the word about Wendlebury events), and at Hector's House.

The weather continued to be mild dry, though chilly, so we expected a good turn-out. The Wendlebury Writers arrived at the Village Hall early as we all had specific tasks to do before the event could start. I opened the stage curtains and moved the oak lectern up onto the stage, while Dinah switched on the stage lighting and Bella tested the microphone. On a long table at the back of the hall, Julia and Louisa set out wine glasses and bottles of sparkling wine and mineral water. Karen found a basket for donations for the refreshments and added a float. Jessica set up a whiteboard on an easel at the bottom of the stage steps, and wrote at the top the running order of the authors whose work we'd be reading. She left the marker pen in place so members of the audience who wanted to perform could add their chosen authors' names after ours. Then we all set out rows of chairs for the audience.

By the time the first reading was due to start, the list was a dozen authors long. I was pleased to see most of the Wendlebury Players in the audience. A couple of them were planning to read, and I hoped this evening's event would provide a nice, gentle way for them to get back on the acting bicycle after falling off, so to speak, following Linda's murder.

At work during the day, I'd tried to persuade Hector to take a turn. After all, he was very good at recommending authors and books for people to read. But he declined, saying he'd prefer to swell the numbers in the audience.

"*They also serve who only stand and wait*," he pronounced, in a manner that made me think it might be a famous quote. I was glad I thought to Google it on my phone when he wasn't looking, thus saving myself the embarrassment of replying that it was kind of him to volunteer to be our wine waiter. As it turned out, it was me who did the waiting, as he was one of the last to arrive.

The Wendlebury Writers sat in the front row, and as I turned to look for Hector, I spotted another familiar face in the audience – the Reverend Neep, sitting offputtingly close to the stage at the end of the row behind me. This row was otherwise empty, although the seats behind were almost all taken.

What normal person ever sits right at the front of an event, given the choice?

When Hector finally arrived, I saw him notice Neep, and sit in the back row to be as far from him as possible.

The Writers had decided to perform in chronological order by author's date of birth, which put me in fourth place on the bill, after Jessica's Elizabeth Barrett Browning, Jacky's Charles Dickens and Bella's Robert Frost. I had eight years on Louisa as Agatha Christie. After my reading of the passage from *Mrs Dalloway* of Clarissa choosing flowers in Miss Pym's florist's shop (*"There were flowers: delphiniums, sweet peas, bunches of lilac; and carnations, masses of carnations…"*), I sneaked back to sit by Hector, and was glad when he smiled and reached for my hand to give it an approving squeeze. I needn't have been so nervous.

After Dinah, the last of the Writers to perform, had delivered her Sylvia Plath piece, we had a brief interval for drinks. Hector fetched us each a glass of sparkling wine. He raised his in a toast to me.

"The drinks may not be up to the standard they had at Mrs Dalloway's party," he said, "but then she wasn't partying in Wendlebury Village Hall."

Then it was the turn of the six guest readers to perform their chosen pieces in the order they'd written their authors' names on the board. While we were waiting for everyone to settle back in their seats, Hector appraised the second half of the programme.

"I see Shakespeare's rubbing shoulders with Jerome K Jerome, but I don't think either of them would mind. P G Wodehouse, Jane Austen – all a bit predictable. Ian Rankin – no surprise there. But Goethe? How interesting. I wonder who's chosen him?"

Having visited the Goethe Museum in Düsseldorf when I was working in Germany, I racked my brains as to what I could remember about him so that I could say something intelligent at the end. Then we sat back to enjoy the readings. The first five were carried out with reasonable competence and accuracy. Ian gave a surprisingly convincing impression of Bertie Wooster, and Mary's extract from Shakespeare entranced me with its thyme and oxlips and nodding violets. I was just thinking Shakespeare might make a good alternative if my nativity play didn't work out, when Hector reminded me this was Titania's speech from *A Midsummer Night's Dream*, so I decided to keep it up my sleeve for summer use.

I knew the first five readers by sight at least, and was wondering who the Goethe fan would be when the vicar got to his feet.

"I would never have put him down as a lover of German poetry," I whispered to Hector.

"Wagner, perhaps," he hissed back, frowning.

In my head I tried to channel Joshua's charitable attitude. Surely it was a good sign that Mr Neep was trying to fit in with the villagers now, listening politely to the other readers and taking his turn on an equal footing, instead of throwing his weight about.

He stood proudly at the lectern, shoulders back, head held high, in his comfort zone, as if in the pulpit. After panning the audience to make sure he had their full attention, he drew a small black cloth-covered book from his jacket pocket, opened it at an early page, and began to read in loud, resonant tones.

"*'The two angels arrived at Sodom in the evening, and Lot was sitting in the gateway of the city'.*"

It didn't sound much like Goethe to me, even in translation – more like a shaggy dog story of the "two men walked in to a bar" variety. Then I realised that he was reading a passage about Sodom and Gomorrah. Even I'd heard of that Bible story. By implication, he was condemning our village, warning us against our own corruption.

Glancing again at the whiteboard, I realised with horror that the last name on the list of authors, scrawled in a spidery hand beneath Ian Rankin, was not the poet Goethe but "God", with rather a lot of decorative flourishes. Mr Neep was reading from the Bible.

A consummate performer, he made constant eye contact with the audience, polling the room like a pro, before singling Hector and Dinah out for special attention. He must have picked up on the grapevine that each of them was gay. Not that Hector was, of course, but for a long time Carol had mistaken his preferences, and he'd allowed her to carry on uncorrected to deflect her affections from him. Carol's unofficial "free gossip with every purchase" policy may have led others in the village to believe it too, and any of them could have told the vicar.

When the vicar came to the end of his reading, he snapped the book shut with a flourish and returned it to his pocket. Nobody clapped, although they had for all the other performers. That didn't upset Neep. I suppose vicars aren't used to applause at the end of a sermon. As he descended the wooden stage steps to resume his seat in the second row, the audience sat in stunned silence.

I glanced sideways at Hector to see how he was taking it. I knew much of the Bible counted as poetry, and wondered whether there was hidden beauty in this passage that had passed me by. In the dim auditorium light, I could see his expression was of open disdain.

Dinah was first to gather her wits, returning to the stage to invite all the readers to take a bow, and thanking everyone for coming. After that, we all flocked towards the wine, except for the vicar, who stalked out of the door into the darkness.

"What a shame that he had the last slot of the night, because he rather stole everyone's thunder," said Julia after the Writers had all clinked glasses in mutual congratulation.

I passed around a basket of crisps. "Even so, I'm glad I didn't have to follow him," I said. "He killed the atmosphere stone dead. He's like the opposite of a warm-up man."

Jessica looked thoughtful. "I wonder whether he'll come back next term, when we'll be reading pieces we've written ourselves? I wonder what sort of thing he might write?"

I shuddered. "Horror stories, for sure!"

I felt a hand on my shoulder and jumped, assuming that the vicar had returned and heard my remark. I swivelled round, wondering how to put a positive spin on what I'd just said. To my relief, it wasn't Mr Neep at all, but Carol.

"Well done, girls." She stood in silence for a moment, unusually reticent, then blurted out nervously, "Doesn't Mr Neep read well?"

Dinah pulled a face. "Never mind the performance, what a ridiculous passage to choose. Does he really think he's going to win anyone's hearts and minds that way?"

"I gather he was once married," said Jessica, whose contribution to the evening had been a sweetly romantic poem by Elizabeth Barrett Browning.

"Can you imagine what that courtship must have been like?" Dinah's look of dread made us all laugh, except Carol, who blushed and headed off in the direction of the ladies'.

To my relief, I spotted Hector coming towards me bearing two glasses of wine and the excuse I needed to break away from the group. He appeared to be studying my dove-grey shoes. They were a little on the tight side, as May's feet were smaller than mine, but the soft suede was very forgiving. Then his eyes travelled up my cornflower blue tights before settling on my drop-waisted dress.

"It's the same costume that I wore on the float," I said as he handed me a glass.

"Yes, I remember," he said, though I bet he didn't. Men never remember things like that. Damian, my ex-boyfriend, couldn't have described a single item in my wardrobe after we'd been together for seven years.

I shifted uncomfortably from foot to foot under his gaze. "Don't you think it's strange that everyone in this village seems to spend half their time dressed up as someone else? That's not exactly normal, is it? It's amazing none of us ever get mistaken for other people. You'd better look out when you're the Beast for Halloween. People might think you're Billy."

"Now, now, that's no way to talk about our best customer."

"He was the best of customers, he was the worst of customers..." For that erudite jest I had to thank Jacky, who, dressed as Charles Dickens, had read the opening lines of *A Tale of Two Cities*. I'd made a mental note to read the rest of it some time. It sounded all right.

"That's the thing, though, Sophie. We're not judgmental in the way the vicar is. In Wendlebury, we take people as they are. Going around criticising everyone is not the way to endear yourself to the community. And he's doing it in spades."

Dinah nodded. "You're right there, Hector. If Billy had turned up in a cocktail frock and stilettos and read James Joyce's *Ulysses*, people would have accepted it. The vicar needs to walk a mile in someone else's shoes for a change."

"I'd love to see the vicar in Billy's stilettos." I laughed, thinking of Billy's habitual wellies, rain or shine.

"That's how rumours start," said Hector as Carol returned from the ladies'.

But a jest wasn't enough to mollify Dinah on the warpath. "Well, I wish the vicar would try walking a mile in someone else's shoes, in a straight line in any direction. That would at least get him a mile away from the village. Otherwise, someone else will send him packing before long, and there'll be no shortage of volunteers."

"This being Wendlebury, I'm sure they'll form an orderly queue," said Hector mildly. But no-one rushed to the vicar's defence, not even Carol.

Hector stayed behind after the rest of the audience had left to help me and the Writers clear up. As with any event in the Hall, all traces had to be removed, dishes washed, and chairs and tables stacked in the store cupboard ready for whoever had booked the Hall next. As Hector and I left the Hall together, he took my hand as if it was the most natural thing in the world. We rejoined the High Street in companionable silence. Once we had crossed the road to the bookshop, he paused and turned me to face him, putting his hands gently on my shoulders.

"Do you know, I think we might just have had our first date?"

My squeak of excitement was quickly extinguished by a soft kiss. Then he drew back to speak. "You read very well, by the way. Everyone did. You chose a good passage, too. It was a fine evening's entertainment till the last act put a damper on events."

I sighed. Why did Mr Neep have to spoil everyone's fun all the time?

We quickly said goodnight, then, apart from the squeak of my steps across slippery brown leaves on the pavement, I wandered home in silence, alone in the dark.

11 Poetic Licence

I turned up for work the next day just as Hector was flipping the door sign from 'Closed' to 'Open'. I confess my heart also did a bit of a flip at his welcoming smile.

He held the door open for me to enter. As I hung my coat, scarf and beret behind the counter, I watched him detour to the window display to give our clerical spider a quick slap.

"And good morning to you, vicar."

Here we go again, I thought with a sigh. "Hector, forget about Mr Neep. Just avoid him. It's not as if you have to go to church, and it doesn't sound as if he'll be darkening the shop's door again. It's like my fear of crocodiles. My simple solution: don't go near any crocodiles."

"That's easy for you to say. There aren't any crocodiles in Wendlebury."

"Yes, but no-one's asking you to be Neep's best friend. Just ignore him."

He frowned. "It's not that easy in a community this size, Sophie. '*No man is an island*'."

"No man is in Ireland?"

At my blank look, Hector strode over to the poetry section, opening a collection of poetry by John Donne and reading aloud:

"No man is an island,
Entire of itself,
Every man is a piece of the continent,
A part of the main.
If a clod be washed away by the sea,
Europe is the less.
As well as if a promontory were.
As well as if a manor of thy friend's
Or of thine own were:
Any man's death diminishes me,
Because I am involved in mankind,
And therefore never send to know for whom the bell tolls;
It tolls for thee."

"Oh, an *island*. I see." I joined him by the poetry books and pulled down another volume, which happened to be by Edward Lear. I couldn't help but giggle at the first poem I found. "Here you go, console yourself by thinking of the vicar as The Bong with the Luminous Nose, and he'll seem far less troublesome." I looked up at Hector. "We used to play a game like this at school, telling each other's fortunes by opening books at random."

At last I'd made him smile. "That sounds like witchcraft to me. Just right for Halloween."

"I won't tell the vicar if you won't."

He took the book from me, consulted the contents page and tapped a title. "OK, if you'll be the Pussycat to my Owl." I was just about to grab the book from him to find out whether that was a good thing when a group of school-run mums arrived, this time with a few children in tow. I slipped it back on the shelf and headed over to set up the morning coffees. The mums were in a mood of suppressed hysteria as half-term week was approaching and the mild weather was forecast to break, so Hector turned on some New Age relaxation music to soothe them.

When they'd gone, he called over to me where I was busy clearing the tables. "Speaking of great writers, how's your first parish magazine column shaping up? It's due in today, you know."

I did know, and I had been fervently trying to forget about it. The pleasant evening at the Big Read had been followed by a sleepless night wishing I'd never let Hector persuade me to become a regular contributor. However, Ella had announced in the October issue that my new column "Travels with my Aunt's Garden" would appear from November onwards, so now I was committed. Hector was very supportive, probably because he saw it as another subliminal advert for the bookshop. I was struggling to feel as confident myself, and hadn't yet managed to write a single usable word. Plenty of unusable ones were currently nestling in the paper recycling box at home.

Then, washing up the coffee cups, I had a sudden brainwave.

"I know, why doesn't Ella just print my piece that won the prize in the Village Show? Then I can write a fresh column next month."

I tried to avoid the disappointment in Hector's eyes. "OK, but only if you promise me you'll start working on your December piece straight away. And out of courtesy, you should pop in to school this lunchtime to check that she's happy with that. Don't just email her and assume she approves. It's a tough job editing the parish mag, so don't mess her about."

"OK, Mum." I felt suitably chastised.

As soon as the school lunch bell sounded, I donned my coat to visit Ella.

12 Thank God It's Friday

I'd never been into the school during its lunch hour before. It was much noisier than when the children were in the classroom. Though there were only ninety children in the school, the sound effects from the playground suggested there were several hundred outside in the clear autumn sunshine, all engaged in a shouting competition.

In Ella's office there was relative calm, once she'd despatched a small boy with a plaster on his grazed knee. I explained to her my suggestion for my first ever column in the *Parish News*, without letting on that I didn't have an alternative text.

"I thought it would help remind anyone who read my prize-winning entry on Show Day why you asked me to write a regular column. Then next month I'll start writing from scratch."

To my surprise, Ella put up no resistance to my proposal.

"Fine, that's one less person for me to chase now." She pulled a small notepad out of her handbag and put a tick against my name on a largely unticked list. "Can you ping it across to me by email to save me having to type it up?"

"Sure, as soon as I get home tonight."

Now that I'd stopped worrying about my own problem, I had the leisure to notice that she was not looking happy.

"Not having a good day, Ella?"

"It's that bloody vicar again. He's just been in here telling me he wants to make an important announcement about Halloween in our celebration assembly tomorrow – you know, the service at the end of the school day on Fridays that is open to parents and grandparents. Somehow, I have a suspicion that his announcement will not give us much cause to celebrate. I hardly dare go to the assembly myself."

After she'd been so generous about my lassitude with my column, I wanted to show moral support. "Can anyone come to it? Could I?"

"God, Sophie, yes, please do. We could do with another voice of reason in the audience. Or you could just bring gin."

And so on Friday afternoon at half past two, I took a seat at the back of the school hall with the various parents, grandparents, carers and pre-school-age siblings who had come to join the traditional end-of-week-service. Ella had primed me to expect an innocuous, upbeat parade of children showing off prizes and achievements, and a sharing of house points and birthdays. On special occasions a guest might be invited to give a brief talk to the children, but in this case the vicar had asked himself. He'd been reluctant to outline exactly what he planned to say, but the Head, Mrs Broom, had told Ella to let him have carte blanche.

"After all, what harm can a vicar do?" she'd asked.

When all the school announcements had been made and the happy birthdays wished and sung, the vicar was invited to speak. He stalked to the front of the hall from where Mrs Broom had been leading the service, and launched into his message.

"I understand that in years gone by the village of Wendlebury Barrow has seen fit to celebrate Halloween. But as the new spiritual guide of your community, it is my duty of care to advise you to reconsider. Do you know what Halloween really means, children?"

He paused, panning the rows of small children sitting cross-legged in front of him. Welcoming the opportunity for audience participation, they shouted out a few speculative answers.

"Sweets."

"Treats."

"Fancy dress."

"Being sick."

"The man next door frightening Mummy."

"Having to help my little brother cross the road."

The vicar continued as if they had remained silent.

"It means, my children, that you are colluding with the Devil – the very enemy we are trying to defeat. Halloween is the worship of Satan. And begging for sweets from your neighbours turns them into enablers of gluttony, donning the robes of iniquity—"

"Please, sir, what's an iquity?" came a voice from within the top class. Miss Walker, the teacher in charge of literacy, frowned as she scribbled down the words she'd have to explain to the children later. The Vicar's opaque speech had already lost the younger children, who were gazing out of the window, twiddling their hair, or tickling those sitting in front of them. Two of the tiniest in the front row had fallen asleep, propped up against each other. One of them was very gently snoring.

"We all know the evils of sugar, don't we, mothers and fathers? We've all read about the government's proposed sugar tax?" Casting God and the government on the same side was an interesting strategy. Mr Neep became more animated, pacing back and forth across the width of the hall, like a spider frantically spinning a web to trap a passing cloud of flies. Some of the children in the front row became distressed, probably fearing he would tread on them. One started to cry. Impervious as he was, Mr Neep realised he needed to cut to the chase and resort to plain speaking for once.

"A school founded by the church is no place for Satanic rites. So there will be no Halloween celebrations in school this year."

At this clear pronouncement, enough gasps went up from around the hall to create a temporary shortage of oxygen, but unfortunately not enough to silence Mr Neep. He reiterated.

"None of the trappings of the modern Halloween, either. No trick-or-treating. No decorations. No costumes. And the PTA Halloween Disco is cancelled."

Rumblings of discontent quickly rose to a roar of protest, peppered by wails from some of the children.

"But we loves our Halloween Disco."

"These nippers don't do no harm asking for sweets. Gets them off the Xbox for the night."

"But what am I to do with all these lollies I've just bought in?"

"What about the money the disco raises for the PTA?"

Some of the parents got up from their seats, gesturing at the vicar and shaking their fists. The vicar took a few steps back, bumping into the piano behind him. He steadied himself against it, apparently surprised at the upset his ruling had caused.

The objections increased in volume until Mrs Broom took charge. She'd been sitting at the side of the hall during the vicar's speech, but now returned to stand beside him and held up her hands for silence. She was in a difficult position, having to report to him as he was a school governor, but needing to keep her school community happy, not least the PTA.

"Now, now, children, mums, dads, grannies, grandads – I'm sure the vicar's not saying this lightly, are you, Mr Neep? I assume you have a better plan in store? After all, you wouldn't like to disappoint your new congregation, would you?"

I could see why she'd been made a headmistress.

Mr Neep took a few steps forward again. "Mrs Brush, you assume correctly." He sounded to me as if he was playing for time. "Of course, I'll be glad to offer an alternative diversion. There will be an excellent All Souls' Day service in the church on November the second." He scanned the adults to gauge whether that would be sufficient compensation, but they just muttered contemptuously to each other. I wondered how much experience he'd had with Jedis. "Of course, four days later it will be time to celebrate Guy Fawkes' Night."

"Guy Forks Knives? What's that, Mrs Broom?" This came from one of the younger children.

Mrs Broom smiled indulgently and turned to the vicar. "I'm afraid we haven't marked Guy Fawkes' Night in Wendlebury for years, Mr Neep. Health and safety, you know. If the PTA were to stage a bonfire party, we'd have to pay more for insurance than we could hope to raise in admissions. We simply daren't risk lighting fireworks in the presence of small children in our school field. If families want to see a firework display, they go to the big one at Slate Green."

Mr Neep looked as if he considered he had won.

"My dear Mrs Brush, you are missing the opportunity for political education there. Think of the fun of burning Guy Fawkes in effigy, celebrating his failed attempt to blow up our Houses of Parliament and impose the evils of Catholicism on our country."

"You want us to burn someone at the stake?" asked one of the mums. "I don't call that very Christian."

"That's terrorism, that is!" said another.

The lady sitting next to me whispered, "It'll give the kids nightmares if we start setting fire to people. They get enough of that on the telly."

Mrs Broom came forward again. "I'm sorry, Mr Neep, but we simply can't celebrate Guy Fawkes' Night in school. Think of the risk assessment I'd have to do. There's none of that to worry about with the Halloween Disco."

An elderly gentleman in the back row waved his walking stick for attention.

"I'd rather have my grandson go round the houses asking for sweets than sitting on the pavement asking for a Penny for the Guy like we did in my day. And it wouldn't be pennies they'd be asking for, either. Pennies don't go nowhere these days. They'd be tapping us for folding money. Much cheaper to give 'em enough lollipops on Halloween to shut 'em up for the week."

"We don't want to wait till Christmas for our next PTA Disco," said one glamorous-looking mum standing at the back. I could imagine her throwing provocative shapes on the dance floor.

"Or miss out on the fundraising," said a dad in a business suit.

But the vicar would not be gainsaid. He raised his hand to stop their protests in mid-flow. "Do not trouble yourself, Mrs Brush. The Guy Fawkes' Night party will be at the vicarage. The diocesan insurance will cover all eventualities."

Ella, responsible for the school's insurance, shot me a doubtful look, muttering, "What about acts of God?"

But the vicar hadn't finished yet. Mrs Broom returned to her seat to let him have the floor once more.

"You are all invited. You are all welcome as my guests. However, this generous invitation is offered provided that you don't disobey me and mark Halloween. There must be no Halloween celebrations in any school for which I'm responsible. My children, I say this only for your own good. I have your best interests at heart. Because I care about you. So no dressing up in Halloween costumes, or you may get mistaken for a guy and get burned on my bonfire, ha ha."

Nearly everyone gasped again, but Mr Neep steamrollered on. He looked from one child to another around the room as the adults exchanged dubious glances. "Because my mission at this school is to keep you all on the path of righteousness. Should you stray, I have it on the highest authority of the good Lord above that when your turn comes to depart this life, you will burn eternally."

"What's a ternally?" The vocabulary-curious child from earlier triggered sniggers from the grown-ups. "Is it one of those big candles from Ikea?"

One grey-haired grandmother put up her hand. "Do we need to bring food, vicar? Or fireworks?"

"Or booze?" asked a dad. Mr Neep looked pleased, as if he'd found the way to their hearts at last. "No, no, all will be supplied. Food, drink, and fireworks will all be served up in abundance."

"So much for fostering abstinence," I whispered to Ella, although looking at the vicar's lean frame, I suspected his idea of abundance was different to mine.

When the vicar finally sat down, Mrs Broom stood up to make a final address. "Well, children, mums and dads, grannies and grandads, well done for another wonderful week. Now go away and have a restful and relaxing half-term break. Come back to school refreshed and ready to share another busy and exciting term's learning."

Along with the rest of the adult guests, I stayed in my seat while the children filed out of the hall. The vicar and the Head disappeared in the direction of Mrs Broom's office. In the absence of any figures of authority, the conversation at the back of the hall immediately rose to playground volume.

"I heard the old duffer's teetotal," one of the dads was saying. "I bet his free drinks won't be worth having. It'll be glasses of squash all round, I reckon."

"I don't call that a party," said another. "Besides, what about our lovely Halloween costumes? We can't wear those on bonfire night. Most of them are nylon. We'd go up in flames at the slightest spark. We can still let the kids trick-or-treat away from school, so long as they don't call in at the vicarage. So we can still do most of Halloween, just not the disco. And then enjoy the vicar's fireworks party the following week."

"With the addition of a little firewater, perhaps." One of the dads gave a sly wink as he mimed drinking from an imaginary bottle. "He doesn't need to know. We just won't give any to him."

"Shame about losing the disco, though," said a dark-haired lady. "That means the PTA will miss out on the ticket sales and the bar profits."

"We don't get many opportunities for a good bop in this place," said one of her friends.

"We could always make the PTA a few quid by running a sweepstake, like we do for the Grand National," said a dad. "Whose guy burns first, fastest, slowest, last. There are plenty of possibilities – £1 a ticket, £20 to the winner, and the rest to the PTA."

"That's a bit ghoulish," said somebody's gran. "Like the ancient Romans seeing which Christian will be first to be eaten by the lions. But my money's on my little grandson."

Still plotting, the adults departed into the playground, ready to collect their children to go home.

I followed Ella back to her office, pausing only for her to tug on the rope to ring the school bell for the end of the day. There were already a couple of parents waiting at her office door, probably to complain about the vicar, so I thought it better to take my leave, said goodbye and wandered despondently out of the building, putting on my coat.

13 Right Guy, Right Place

"Please don't shoot the messenger, Hector. I'm just telling you so you can be prepared."

I tried to find a positive spin on events.

"Maybe we could buy in some history books about Guy Fawkes, and make a display in the window to draw attention to them. I bet most modern kids don't know much about the Gunpowder Plot."

Hector blinked thoughtfully, then clapped his hands as if the problem was solved.

"You're right. I have never liked Guy Fawkes' Night. The whole sorry episode was hardly England's finest hour. Commemorating it just propagates animosity between faiths. That's the last thing we need more of in today's society. But I suppose we could add a modern slant to promote it as a cautionary tale."

As I came round behind him to hang my coat up, I was pleased to see him start searching our suppliers' database for books about Guy Fawkes.

To my surprise, the parents and children who came into the shop a few minutes later on the way home from school seemed reasonably happy with the vicar's proposal.

"Have you got any books about this guy Mr Fawkes, Hector?" asked a little boy. "My mum said she'll buy me a sticker book of him if you've got one."

"Are there are any colouring sheets with bombfires on them?" asked a little girl, sitting down at the play table in the tearoom.

"Bonfires," said her mother, rooting through our pile of seasonal colouring sheets. Finding none, she turned over a witch picture to provide a blank sheet and picked out red, orange and yellow crayons from the box. "You'll have to draw your own. Good girl."

Hector went out to the stockroom, returning a few moments later with cellophane sheets in fiery shades – protective packaging from some expensive art books we'd taken delivery of earlier that week. From behind the counter he produced glue sticks and safety scissors.

"Here, cut these sheets up to make a collage of a bonfire, and I'll put the best ones on the wall." He reached behind the tearoom counter to grab a couple of empty cardboard coffee capsule sleeves. "There you go, you can use these to make the logs."

"Just what we need in this village, trainee arsonists," he said so quietly that only I could hear, but at least he was smiling as he passed the cardboard to a little girl.

Having completed the orders for tea and coffee, I was about to start dusting the bookshelves when the shop door creaked and Joshua teetered in, accompanied by a blast of cold wind.

"Ah, hello, my dear. I hear the weather's about to take a turn for the worse, so I decided to go for a constitutional before the rain starts."

He crossed slowly to the tearoom. One of the mums removed her handbag from the last spare chair to allow him to sit down. The children all knew Joshua, as he led the Carnival Parade every year at the Village Show, marching smartly in his best tweed suit and velvet bow tie from the village green to the showground. Watching him teeter across the shop now, I realised the procession might have to slow down next year so as not to overtake him.

A little girl took her picture over to show him, perhaps wise to his reputation for slipping sugar lumps from the bowls on the table to small children who took the time to talk to him.

"Do you like my firebomb picture, Mr Hampton?" she asked sweetly. Joshua shot an alarmed glance to her mother.

"Bonfire, darling."

Joshua laughed. "Ah, a bonfire. Gunpowder, treason and plot. Lovely, my dear. Now, can you draw a nasty old Guy Fawkes sitting on top of it?"

The little girl gave him such a lingering quizzical look that I thought she might be about to use him as a model. I stuffed my duster in the back pocket of my jeans and went over to watch the artist at work.

"I suppose you did all that sort of thing when you were little, Joshua? Bonfire night? Making a guy so you could go begging for a Penny for the Guy, and all that?"

Joshua nodded. "Ah, yes, so much nicer than this modern Halloween business, which always seems disrespectful of the church tradition. I much prefer the second of November. All Souls' Day is about remembering and respecting your long-lost loved ones, not making death something to fear."

I could understand that philosophy in an eighty-six-year-old like Joshua, but it seemed unfair to make little ones remember dead people. The biggest bereavement most of them had experienced would have been the loss of a pet.

"Whereas Guy Fawkes' Night was harmless fun, and of course we spun it out for several days, making our guys the week before. The task was not much different to making scarecrows, building an effigy by filling old clothes with straw and newspaper. We took delight in drawing on the kind of beards and moustaches they sported in the days of the Gunpowder Plot." He stroked his chin. "Little pointed beards, you know, like the Cavaliers. We couldn't always get the clothes to make a guy, though. They were on ration. Dear me, no. 'Make do and mend' was my mother's motto. She'd have had forty fits if we'd put clothes on a guy that had any wear left in them. Not even a bit of sacking. That would be turned into a rag rug. Sometimes we had to improvise our guys out of nothing but branches and leaves."

"What, like a wicker man?" Hector sounded impressed.

Joshua nodded. "We may not have had the material goods these youngsters have nowadays, but we knew how to have fun. We used to take them to sit on the pavement outside the pub and ask for a Penny for the Guy as our reward. You could get a banger for a penny in those days." He noticed the children looking puzzled. "A banger is a very small firecracker. You light one end, throw it on the ground, and it jumps about all over the place in a shower of sparks. We'd chase each other down the High Street with them. Such larks! Every penny I got for my guy went on bangers. And we always had a cracking bonfire on the green to burn our guys on."

A couple of the mums exchanged anxious glances. Surreptitiously I counted Joshua's fingers, to make sure he had grown up intact.

Some boys from the top class started crumpling bits of coloured cellophane. Its crackling sounded surprisingly like real fire.

"Sophie, please may we have some silver foil off the cakes? We're making a model."

I passed them a few empty foil cupcake cases that I'd just washed to put in the recycling. "Here you go. And here's a cardboard cake box you can use as a base."

By the time their mums had drunk their coffee, the children had presented Hector with a recognisable miniature bonfire and were imploring him to put it in the window. Hector returned a few Halloween books to the shelves to make room for it.

"Now all you need is a guy," said Joshua, nodding approval on his way to the front door. "And Handel's 'Firework Music'."

Obediently Hector curtailed Saint-Saens's '*Danse Macabre*', which he'd designated as our default Halloween soundtrack, and clicked on Joshua's requested piece. As the first notes resonated around the shop, I thought how atmospheric the music was – an overture to excitement yet to come.

"You can borrow one of my Action Men to be a guy, if you like, Hector," said one of the boys. "But you won't really burn him, will you? I will get him back after it's all over, won't I?"

"I sincerely hope so," Hector said solemnly, holding the door open for Joshua, "unless pyromania breaks out in the village."

"Pirate what?"

"Never you mind," said the boy's mum.

Resisting the temptation to put the Action Man in a vicar's outfit, I decided to call in to the village shop on my way home to ask Carol to knock up a tiny Guy Fawkes costume. I didn't want to fan the flames of Hector's relationship with the vicar. If there were going to be any fiery feelings in this shop, I wanted them to be strictly between Hector and me.

14 Penny For Them

When we opened the shop on Saturday morning, the clerical spider was still watching over us from where he was suspended in the shop window. I hoped he would not bring us bad luck for the last weekend before Halloween, because we still had masses of stock to shift.

However, I needn't have worried. As the day went by, more and more customers came in to buy ghost stories, spooky stickers and creepy colouring books. Some parents told me they were planning to celebrate Halloween at home. Others would be allowing their children to trick-or-treat, but only if they promised to avoid the vicarage. As all the parents compensated their children for any disappointment by spending more on Halloween goods at the bookshop than they otherwise might have done, Hector's mood lightened.

When I called in to see Carol on the way home that evening, she was experiencing the same effect.

"I haven't done so badly after all. There's still over a week to go, but I've sold a lot of costumes and trick-or-treat sweets. I'm just sad not to have the chance of meeting that special someone at the disco."

I was feeling sorry for myself on that score too. Although I still had my night out with Hector to look forward to on Guy Fawkes' Night the following Saturday, we'd miss the opportunity for an earlier date.

The only one who seemed to have welcomed the vicar's ruling was Joshua, buoyed up by fond memories of burning past guys. When he knocked on my back door next morning to bring me a couple of late cooking apples from his tree, he had further developments to report.

"I see the Reverend Neep has put up posters around the village inviting everyone to his free fireworks party," he said. "It's very generous of him. He certainly seems eager to please the youngsters."

I took the apples from him, set them on the table, and turned to fill the kettle.

"Don't you think it's a bit odd how adamant Mr Neep is about Halloween? I mean, I know he's a vicar, but I didn't think they made them like that any more. He's a throwback to fire-and-brimstone puritanical times. He's like someone who's never met a vicar doing an impression of one."

Joshua settled down in his usual chair.

"My dear, am I right to assume you've not spent much time in the company of vicars?" He had a point. I knew Joshua could draw on his decades of experience as a member of the Parochial Church Council. "In any case, it's not for us to criticise the vicar. We must trust the judgement of the diocese to appoint the best man for the job."

"So you think Mr Neep is the best man they could get? I suppose these things are relative." I shuddered to think of what the rejects might have been like. It had crossed my mind that Neep might have bought himself a vicarship, like you can buy phoney Scottish lairdships or degrees online. Or he might have been the only applicant.

I spooned loose tea into the pot.

"There will be a party line from the church, but each vicar may add his own personal touch, playing to his special strengths. We should support Mr Neep's new ventures and encourage our fellow parishioners to interact with him in as positive a way as we can, for the good of the community."

Wondering whether the vicar's special strength was arson, I hoped the vicarage was well-equipped with fire extinguishers.

15 Poster Campaign

The following morning, on the way to work, I spotted the vicar's hand-drawn signs announcing his fireworks party, all in capital letters. They were pinned to every telegraph pole along the High Street, where previously there had been PTA Halloween Disco posters. I tried to look at them positively for Joshua's sake, admiring the time and trouble Mr Neep had taken to spread the word, even if his artwork was appalling. His lettering looked shaky and uneven, like a ransom note in which the kidnapper has tried to hide his identity. The chilly drizzle, the first rain we'd had for a couple of weeks, was sending the ink into little rivulets down the page.

Included were details of the guy competition. Entrants were invited to bring their guy to the vicarage by 5pm on the fifth of November so that the vicar could judge them. They should return with their families at 7.30pm for the grand lighting ceremony, followed by a firework display.

When a smattering of children, shiny and dripping in their waterproofs and wellingtons, came into Hector's House that afternoon, they were buzzing with excitement about the contest. Their mothers, shaking the rain off their umbrellas before leaving them in the bucket by the door, were less enthusiastic.

"Honestly, Sophie, we spend our lives trying to teach our kids to steer clear of matches, then along comes Mr Neep inviting them to set fire to things," said one as I set down a cappuccino in front of her. She cast a nervous glance at the play table where her small son was absorbed in colouring a bonfire picture, going way over the lines in his enthusiasm to create a really big fire.

"I suppose that's one reason why we've always preferred having a Halloween Disco to a fireworks party at school," said her friend. "Plus it means we all get to stay in the warm."

I brought over the cakes they'd ordered and set them on the table. "What will you do about it?"

"Well, they all want to enter the competition now, so we can't stop them," said the first mother. "They're treating it like homework, as the vicar first told them about it at school."

"I've never seen my son so eager to do homework in half-term before," said the other. "Oh well, at least the vicar's party won't cost us anything. Which is more than could be said for Halloween. I always spend a fortune on decorations, costumes and sweets."

The other nodded. "Yes, and it'll save us traipsing down to Slate Green to see the council's display, which means we don't have to worry about drinking and driving."

They both perked up. "And there's not many homeworks that positively encourage parents to drink. So maybe it won't be so bad after all."

When the mums returned to comparing notes about the previous night's television programmes, I left them to it.

I thought it wise to call in at the village shop on the way home to make sure Carol kept her stocks of matches well out of reach of small children, selling them only to responsible adults. I had yet to be convinced that the latter included the vicar.

16 In the Company of Angels

After work the following Thursday, I was due to attend the weekly meeting of the Wendlebury Players to update them on the progress of my script for their winter production.

Whatever they had been expecting, I knew it wasn't what I was about to propose, so I ran the idea past Hector at work that morning for reassurance. He knew the members of the Players better than Ella or I did, so would be a better gauge of their likely reaction.

"So you see, it would kill two birds with one stone," I said. "I can write a straight nativity play with the adults playing the roles the children would normally take, and choreograph the little ones into cute animal scenes."

Hector looked dubious. "I hope you aren't building up to a production of *Jesus Christ, Superstar* for Easter? Please don't stretch our willing suspension of disbelief by asking the five women players to play twelve male disciples."

"What about the parable of the loaves and the fishes?" Billy was enjoying his elevenses in the far corner of the tearoom, unperturbed by the aroma of wet dog arising from his gently steaming tweed jacket. "Cast Ian as Jesus, and he can make them multiply."

"There'll be no shortage of actors because the school staff are going to join in too," I said. "Ella Berry has agreed to be the Innkeeper, and the Head is going to be the Angel Gabriel."

"That ain't right," said Billy. "Mrs Broom's a woman and the Angel Gabriel's a man."

"No, the Angel Gabriel's a woman, though I agree it's an odd name for a girl. Angels should be called things like Celeste."

When I glanced at Hector for confirmation, I was surprised to see him looking as if he'd just seen a ghost.

"Hector, aren't all angels women?"

"But not all women are angels," said Billy.

Hector cleared his throat. "Angels are neutral. There's no sex in heaven."

"Then I'm not going," said Billy.

"No change of plan there then," said Hector. "And besides, it's a Bible story, not a Disney film. The names weren't chosen for glamour. Anyway, if heaven's full of the likes of Neep, I'm not going either."

I laughed. "You talk as if your destination after death is optional, like booking tickets at the travel agent. Doesn't God have a say in the matter?"

"I bet if you asked the vicar to take the part of God in your play, he'd say yes," said Billy.

"Isn't he trying to play God already?" said Hector, detouring to the window display to give the spidery Neep a cat-and-mouse swipe.

I tried to turn the focus back on our discussion. "I don't need a God, Billy."

Billy snorted. "Don't you go letting the vicar hear you say that. He thinks you're evil enough already."

Eventually I ascertained that they both liked my idea for the play and anticipated that the prospective cast would too. I left work that evening positively looking forward to presenting the idea to the Players.

17 Dramatic Revelations

When I breezed into the Village Hall that evening, shaking the drizzle off my umbrella, I found the cast awaiting me expectantly, sitting on chairs arranged in a circle like some kind of pow-wow.

I clicked my umbrella open and set it down on the floor to dry by the empty seat they'd saved for me, sat down, and peeled a few dead brown oak leaves off the soles of my shoes. They'd made my wet footprints across the hall floor look a very funny shape, as if I had furry feet.

"Not superstitious then, Sophie?" asked Ian, casting a disapproving glance at my umbrella. I hoped he wasn't going to blame me for any subsequent misfortune. I offered up a silent prayer to the god I didn't believe in that the Players would be as receptive to my proposition as Ella had been.

When I'd unveiled my plan, Ian was first to express enthusiasm. "I always wanted to be Joseph at school, and never got the chance. I bet I can get Stanley to lend us his donkey if you'd like one."

Mary was also delighted. I could tell the other women had been hoping for the Virgin's part, but as I explained, it would make things a lot easier for the children if someone they already knew as Mary played Mary. The three wise men were compensated by the prospect of exotic costumes and sparkly headdresses, and the shepherd happened to be very fond of small children, so was happy to herd the infants as lambs.

"At that age, it'll be more like herding kittens," she said brightly, "but that won't matter as they'll all look so sweet."

With the casting settled, we spent the rest of the evening mapping out the scenes, with the Players enjoying getting into character and improvising lines, leaving me little to do by way of scriptwriting. I used the voice recorder on my phone to make sure I didn't miss anything.

"That was such fun, Sophie," said Mary as we put away the chairs at the end of the meeting. "All we need now is a new Director, and we'll be back on track."

I stopped short of volunteering to direct, but by now I was on a roll, enjoying the post of the Players' saviour.

"Just leave it to me, Mary. I'll get Carol to put up a notice in the shop tomorrow, and ask Ella to give a shout-out in the next parish mag, and we'll announce the vacancy on the bookshop website too."

Between those three resources, I was confident we'd find at least one suitable candidate.

The moment I got home, I started drafting the advert at my desk while the detail was still fresh in my mind. "Vicars need not apply" I put at the end, just in case Mr Neep took it in to his head to do so, then reluctantly crossed it out. I thought it better not to alienate him any further.

18 The Surprise Party

After spending much of Friday at work thinking about my script, and the evening at home writing it, I slept so soundly that for once I awoke refreshed before the alarm clock went off. I could see Hector was surprised when I turned up on time at the shop on Saturday morning.

The day sped past with plenty of customers for both the tearoom and the bookshop. There'd been no chance for the children to let off steam in the village play park, so the mums were glad that we'd laid on so many free activities each day during the wet half-term to keep the children occupied. By the end of the afternoon, we'd sold not only all our Halloween stock, but also a large number of Guy Fawkes history books, and our tearoom takings had quadrupled. Hector asked me to place a new order for Monday. I almost felt bad that we would be missing the vicar's party for our date now.

As I marched swiftly home that evening, the rain was falling like iron railings, and I was glad of the chance for a moment in the dry when Carol beckoned me into the village shop. Usually it closes later than Hector's House, but she'd already locked the door and dimmed the lights. She lifted the latch to let me in, quickly closed the door behind me and spoke in a confidential whisper even though there were no other customers present.

Even in the dim light provided by the fire exit sign and the street light shrouded in mist outside, I could see Carol, unusually flushed, could hardly contain her excitement. "I've just heard the PTA Halloween Disco is back on!" she hissed triumphantly. "Good old Stanley's said we can hold it in his barn. It starts at 7.30 tonight, finishing at midnight as usual. The vicar need never know, as it's out of sight and earshot of the vicarage, and there's no road access, only footpaths and dirt tracks. He's unlikely to go past it by chance, especially after dark. I mean, he's not going to be wandering lonely as a clown across the fields on a wet night like this, is he?"

I knew the barn she meant. It was the one where we'd prepared the Wendlebury Writers' float for the carnival, using one of Stanley's two spare trailers. The other one had been taken by the Wendlebury Players. Back in the summer, I'd spent several evenings there as our two groups decorated our floats at either end of the barn, designs kept secret from each other by the wooden partition that divided the barn in two.

"It's a wonder the PTA hasn't thought of using it before," said Carol. "It'll make a great setting for a spooky disco, as there are two separate rooms. One will be used as a bar and the other as the dance floor. Plus there'll be plenty of hay bales for seating, and if any drinks get spilled, it won't matter, not like in the school hall."

"Mightn't it be a bit chilly on a night like this?" I didn't think a barn would have central heating.

"Not if enough villagers pile down there and start dancing. We'll soon get the place warmed up."

I couldn't bring myself to curb her enthusiasm.

"Sounds perfect to me, Carol. And anyway, I shouldn't worry about Mr Neep. He only said that the disco shouldn't take place at the school. He can't ban Stanley from hosting a party on his own land. I take it you're going?"

She nodded enthusiastically. "Ooh, I never miss the Halloween Disco. You have to take your chances at finding romance in this village."

I felt a pang of guilt that I'd homed in on the eligible Hector myself so soon after arriving in the village, even though Carol was closer to his mother's age than his own.

"Anyway, if Mr Neep's not the sort of person who would enjoy a Halloween Disco, maybe he's not the man for you?" I tried to sound encouraging. "Perhaps some tall, dark, handsome stranger will come in and sweep you off your feet."

She still looked crestfallen, so I moved the conversation on to a more positive vein. "So, what costume will you wear, Carol?"

Brightening, she tapped the side of her nose with her finger. "Ah, that would be telling! You'll have to wait and find out!"

I looked forward to the big reveal.

19 The Lion in Autumn

It wasn't until I got home that I remembered my own costume. I'd left it on a hanger in the stockroom at Hector's House, ready to change in to it on Monday morning for the day of Halloween itself. It was handy that Halloween fell at the start of the new term, as our themed day in the shop would give the children something to look forward to after their first day back at school.

I texted Hector to tell him the disco was back on and to ask him if he'd mind dropping my costume down to me, as I'd left my spare keys to the shop in the tearoom. I wondered whether disco music held much appeal for him. Although I knew from all the tracks he played in the shop to match his customers' tastes that his knowledge of music was extensive and eclectic, I had no idea what he liked to listen to for his own pleasure.

While I waited for Hector to respond, I fixed myself a quick sandwich for tea, as I wasn't sure what food would be on offer at the disco. Although I didn't want to admit the vicar might be on to something with his call for abstinence, far more alcohol than I was used to flowed in this village, and I didn't want to risk drinking on an empty stomach.

While I was eating, a flurry of knocks on the door heralded a series of small groups of children in Halloween costumes, trick-or-treating and wishing me a happy Halloween. I was slightly taken aback.

"It's not Halloween till Monday," I observed to the first group.

"We thought if we did our trick-or-treating today during half-term, rather than on actual Halloween during term-time, the vicar wouldn't count it, so we'd still be allowed to go to his fireworks party," said a pint-sized Incredible Hulk. "And anyway, Mum always says it's better not to trick-or-treat on a school night, because if we're sick from eating too many sweets, we're not allowed to go to school for two days because of the bloody forty-eight hour rule."

I suppressed a grin at his impression of his mother. I wasn't sure a tummy full of sweets was the best preparation for a disco either, but doled them out by the handful anyway.

"After we've finished trick-or-treating, we've got to keep our costumes on for the PTA Halloween Disco. Did you know it's back on?"

I nodded. "Yes. I'll see you there."

A few moments later, I heard the children singing outside Joshua's front door. Considering he disliked Halloween, I had to admire the way he had applied his own standards to the festival, but in a kindly way, unlike the vicar. I hoped he was enjoying his serenade.

After the flurry of callers had slowed down, I dashed upstairs to put on some fresh make-up and was just brushing my hair when there was one more knock at the door. I opened it to find a tall, slender lion on my doorstep with a bulging carrier-bag in one hand.

"You shall go to the ball," said a familiar voice.

"Good evening, Hector." I smiled, admiring how well his Beast costume fitted him, even the splendid maned mask. I pulled my ballgown out of the bag and hung it over the bannisters for any creases to drop out, while he wiped his feet dry on the doormat.

I forgot for a moment that he'd never visited me at home before. He surprised me by striding in as confidently as if he owned the place, taking a seat in the armchair nearest the fireplace, removing his Beast mask and white evening gloves and resting them on the hearthrug. I'd not been home long enough to light the fire, which always takes me a while, but he stretched out his legs to put his feet on the fender as comfortably as if the wood-burning stove was blazing merrily.

"Ah, I'd forgotten just how comfortable this seat was!"

"What do you mean?" Had he been sneaking into my cottage in my absence and testing the furniture like a latter-day Goldilocks? Surely he wasn't a Peeping Tom? Perhaps that was the guilty secret he wanted to confess on our Guy Fawkes' Night date. Could that be why the vicar remembered him? Had Mr Neep once been a magistrate in Hector's university town, and he'd tried him for some awful misdemeanour back in his student days? I was reminded of Bertie Wooster on trial for stealing a policeman's helmet. I hoped Hector's crime was nothing more serious than that.

Hector interrupted my thoughts. "I used to come here quite often to visit May. We'd talk for hours about books and things."

I wondered what else he knew about my house. I thought I'd better change the subject.

"Carol's terribly excited about the disco, you know."

Hector pursed his lips. "Yes, she always is. I suppose I'll be in trouble tonight when she sees me dancing with you."

I shook my head. "Don't worry, you're old news. She's got her eye on Mr Neep now, remember. Not that he'll be there."

Hector covered his eyes with one hand in horror. "Good Lord, these small village populations do have their disadvantages. There are never enough single men to go around. Never mind, she'll still have a good time. She's always the life and soul of the dance floor, and she'll enjoy seeing all her costumes put to good use. People make a real fuss of her at the disco out of gratitude for their outfits. She's highly regarded in the village all year round, of course, but I expect you've noticed that already."

I nodded. "And so she should be. But sometimes regards are not enough."

When Hector looked at me sharply, I realised he might be taking my comment as criticism of the slow progress of our relationship.

"Damian," I said quickly. "I was thinking of Damian." Which was true. Then I realised I was digging an even deeper hole by mentioning the ex-boyfriend who had cited every reason I shouldn't leave him except the one I wanted to hear: that he loved me.

I created a diversion by taking my Beauty ballgown from the bannisters and holding it up against my body. "I'd better go and put this on, then."

Hector nodded approval. "You'll need something to wear over it, by the way. The rain's easing off a bit, but it'll be quite nippy walking down through the fields to the barn. I've got my mask and mane to keep me warm, not to mention my frockcoat. You'll need a coat, or at least a shawl."

He stood up to pull down from the shelf above the desk one of May's books, and he settled down to read it while I changed into my costume. I was grateful to leave him engrossed in something that might take his mind off my failed relationship with Damian.

Appraising myself in the long mirror on Auntie May's wardrobe door, I felt like a child playing at dressing up. With the bedroom curtains closed against the night, I was illuminated only by the dim bedside light. I felt like a fairy tale princess.

I scooped up my hair and secured it into a French pleat with Auntie May's mother-of-pearl combs, and added a pair of pearl drop earrings. Then I swept down the narrow staircase as regally as I could, remembering for once not to bang my head on the low beam, returning to my handsome prince as the clock struck a quarter past seven.

117

Hector had already put the book back on the shelf and replaced his lion's mask in preparation to head out of the door as soon as I was ready.

"Sophie, you look stunning." At least, I think that's what he said. His voice was rather muffled by the mask, and I didn't like to ask him to repeat it.

Whisking a red pashmina from the hallstand and wrapping it around my shoulders, I allowed him to lead me out into the night. Pulling the door closed behind me, I dropped my key into the pocket of his frock coat, my own costume being pocketless. As we turned off from the High Street to walk down unlit footpaths, I hoped it was not reckless to stray through dark, silent fields in the company of a lion, even if it was wearing evening dress.

20 The Belle of the Ball

Hand in hand, we crept down through the muddy fields to Stanley's barn. With the moon obscured by cloud, it looked as if glow-worms of all shapes and sizes were quietly descending the hill – or a host of the undead converging on their prey. Illuminated only by the lights they carried, from old-fashioned lanterns to torch apps on mobile phones, the partygoers progressed to the foot of the valley. In the shadow of a small deciduous woodland lay the barn, surrounded by a circle of dirt beaten down by constant tractor traffic, now carpeted with fallen leaves.

The walk down had been slippery, so our splashy progress, interjected by shrieks as I slid about in my red leather ballet flats, had disturbed the nocturnal wildlife. From the woodland below us, a barn owl swooped up the hill towards the churchyard. From behind the barn a fox came leaping, turning to gaze just long enough for us to remark on it, before rushing purposefully off into the woods. Then something sped across the footpath in front of me so fast that I couldn't tell what it was. Although it was tiny, it startled me enough to make me shriek again.

Hector's reassuring tones were muffled by his mask. "Don't worry, Sophie, you're safe with me. The local wildlife won't risk the wrath of a lion."

I wished I too had a full-head mask to stop the damp night air turning my hair frizzy. I was glad to arrive in the halo of light that spilled out of the open barn door.

"Ooh, proper lighting, that's good," I said to Hector. "Do you think there'll be heating too?"

"I hardly think so. They'll have had to bring in a generator for the lights and the disco kit as it is."

I still had so much to learn about country life.

The trailer we had used as our carnival float stood on the far side of the room, transformed into a makeshift bar. Some of its decorations were still on board, such as the backdrop lined with wrapping paper bought from Hector's House, showing the spines of antique books. Replacing the chairs were a couple of shiny metal beer kegs, chunky wine boxes, and small plastic bottles of soft drinks. Stacks of plastic cups meant no-one had to worry about breakages. As at the Village Show, bales of hay provided prickly but sturdy seating, and in every spare space against the wall stood pairs of wellies of all shapes, colours and sizes. I wish I'd thought to carry my dancing shoes and walk down in wellies instead.

Although, thanks to Hector, we arrived on the dot of the official start time, some of the partygoers had already made significant inroads into the supplies of drink, perhaps having started when they were setting up the bar. The only access to the disco floor, from which the "Macarena" was escaping at high volume, was through a low stable door in the partition between the two rooms. The average height of those on the dance floor suggested they were of trick-or-treating age. Hector took one look and led me by the hand to the trailer to buy us drinks.

"Do you want a straw with that, Hector?" asked Stanley, serving him a pint of bitter, noting that the mouth opening in his mask provided enough space to breath but not to sup from a glass.

"How did you know it was Hector?"

No visible part of Hector's body was recognisably his. Stanley nodded indulgently at our still clasped hands. "Of course it's Hector. Who else would it be?"

I'd forgotten about the village grapevine. Billy, who'd interrupted our first kiss, was second only to Carol as a source of gossip. I grinned feebly.

"Well, I'm rather hoping it's Hector in there, anyway." I wondered whether all of Carol's costumes were unique. I'd hate to find myself dancing later with the wrong Beast.

We carried our drinks to an empty bale and sat down to survey the scene. The assembly made an impressive sight, and I was relieved that most of them were not at all scary. Carol seemed to favour the Halloween values of Disney rather than the Brothers Grimm. Even her vampires looked friendly.

Several bookshop regulars stopped to make small talk with us, saying pointedly how glad they were to see me and Hector out together. Clearly none of them considered that the masked man now sitting with one hand on my thigh might be anyone other than him.

I was just starting to bask in the general acceptance of us as an item when I spotted Carol emerging from the dance floor. Slightly breathless, she had "let it go" with the little girls to the popular song of that name from *Frozen*. She sported a long, thick, white, plaited wig and the most beautiful Elsa costume, covered in sequins that twinkled at her every turn. I couldn't help but smile, she looked so happy.

She gave us a cheerful wave and made a beeline for us. Hector, doing a shameful impression of the Cowardly Lion, drained his pint as an excuse to escape to the bar. Carol, unbowed by his action, gratefully threw herself down on to the bale next to me and stretched out her legs.

"Phew, I'm exhorbitant already. I've been dancing non-stop so far."

I smiled. "And so you should be. You are the real Belle of the ball, Carol. Your costume is gorgeous. No wonder you're up on the dance floor showing it off." Now she was closer, I was able to take in the incredible detail of her gown. "That must have taken you weeks."

"Yes, it did. All sewn by hand, too. No effort spared. And the kids love it."

"Well, you're worth every last sequin, Carol."

She slipped off an immaculate pointed shoe, sparkling beneath the disco lights, and bent to rub her toes. She must have walked down in wellies. "That's kind of you to say so, Sophie. I just wish someone else was here to see it."

I cast an urgent glance across to Hector, now deep in conversation with a silver-faced wizard at the bar. Surely she wasn't still carrying a torch for him? She followed my look and shook her head.

"Don't worry, I don't mean your Hector. I gave up on him a long time ago. Even before I realised that you'd converted him."

My mouth dropped open but she continued before I could think of something politically correct to say.

"No, I mean someone who isn't likely to even consider coming here. And to be honest, I'm half hoping he doesn't."

"Not Mr Neep, surely?"

Our conversation was cut short by cries of "Come in, vicar!" near the barn door, accompanied by horrified gasps from those who could not see who it was, and a squeal of enthusiasm from Carol.

Billy, glad as ever to be the centre of attention, came striding into the bar wearing a black jacket and black shirt over his usual corduroy trousers, and a white plastic clerical dog collar. He took the collar off to demonstrate its origins – an old bleach bottle – to the admiring crowd that had gathered around him.

"See, anyone can be a vicar if they want, even me!"

Only Carol seemed disappointed that it wasn't Mr Neep. She sat back and looked pointedly in the opposite direction as Billy did a circuit of the room, high-fiving anyone who cared to admire his home-made costume. Unlike everyone else, he kept his wellies on.

I saw Hector buy Billy his first pint and suspected Billy wouldn't have to pay for any of his own drinks that night.

Billy came over to raise his glass to me, looking smug. "There, young miss, I told you I'd do it. And I didn't even need to buy one of Carol's fancy costumes either."

Carol looked even more deflated, and Billy, sensitive for once, tried to make it up to her.

"But you've both scrubbed up very well tonight, if I may say so." Carol looked only a little consoled. Billy turned his back on us to survey the room. "So, when are they going to turf these kiddiewinks out so the real party can get started?"

Carol explained the usual rules to me. "Generally the children stay till about nine o'clock, dancing to the kind of music they like, then the parents take them home and we move on to more grown-up stuff. You know, 50s, 60s, 70s, 80s, 90s – all the nostalgic records that take people back to their prime."

I thought better than to remind her that, in the 90s, my main source of music was nursery rhymes.

A song that I recognised vaguely as the theme music to a children's television programme struck up in the next room.

"But some of us can waltz to anything. In fact, I think I will." And with that, Carol was gone again, waltzing across the room as a warm-up.

Billy took her place on the bale next to me, noisily slurping on his beer, and told me about the exploits he'd got up to in this barn when he was a lad. These mainly involved a girl called Veronica of whom everybody's parents disapproved, which for Billy counted as a recommendation. I shot an anxious look across to Hector, wondering whether he had abandoned me for the night. Now a shaggy gorilla had buttonholed him at the bar, and he didn't seem to mind at all. So much for my high hopes of a night like Cinderella's, only without the midnight dash.

Making excuses to Billy, I decided to take a tip from Carol. I refused to be downhearted, instead throwing myself into the action. Why wait for the action to come to me, when I could go to it? A bone-chilling gust of air from outside made me shiver, confirming my decision to hit the dance floor, and I headed through the stable door into the heat and light of the disco.

21 Trouble at the Barn

Dancing with Carol was hardly how I'd expected to spend the evening, but with Dutch courage from a second large glass of wine, thrust into my hand by a generous vampire at the edge of the dance floor, I found myself rushing up to join her. Rewarded with her companionable smile, I shimmied about to various childish songs for over an hour before the lights came up and the DJ, one of the dads, announced that it was bedtime. Startled, I wondered whether Wendlebury was a secret haven for wife-swapping until I realised he meant just for the children.

A brief pause in the music followed while they found their coats and their parents. Still buzzing after all the exercise, they were despatched into the cold night air with faces glowing like Rudolph's nose, escorted by either parents or babysitters. The short break in the music prompted any adults still on the dance floor to head to the bar for a much-needed drink.

As I queued to be served, I realised I had no money on me and used this excuse to abandon Carol for Hector. My guilty conscience was assuaged when she was quickly swept up by a couple of other villagers whose costumes bore the hallmark of her handiwork.

To my surprise, Hector was sitting alone on the bale where he'd left me, his mask removed and on his lap. He gave me a slightly sheepish smile as I came towards him.

"What happened to you?"

If he had been Damian, I'd have retorted, "I could ask you the same thing," and we'd have descended into a row. I discarded that option and instead smiled what I hoped was winningly.

"I've been dancing with Carol. I'm puffed." I sat down beside him and gratefully accepted the glass of wine he had waiting for me. "Is it always like this, the Halloween Disco?"

"It's not usually held down here, obviously. It's more civilised in the school hall, warmer and less muddy. But to be fair, the barn has more atmosphere, being surrounded by dark fields and trees rather than the school playground with its security lights. Nor is the barn lined with children's paintings and other school accoutrements at odds with the Halloween theme. But there are the same faces, same tunes, and many of the same costumes."

I took a long draught from my glass. "I'm amazed at how many people I recognise even when they're heavily made up or wearing wigs and masks."

"Sherlock Holmes did say you can never disguise a back, and I think he's right." Hector pointed to a green-haired witch who was drinking beer from a small black cauldron, a plastic snake entwined round its handle. "That's Dinah, for sure. And over there is Ella Berry." He indicated a slim figure completely enveloped in a fluorescent skeleton suit, who turned, waved to me, and gave me an enthusiastic double thumbs-up when she spotted who I was with. "See that mummy propping up the bar? That's the Chair of the PTA, chatting to the Chair of the Board of Governors, Tutankhamen. They must have got together to plan that double act."

"They're not at all scary when you know who they all are, not even the really hideous ones." I motioned to one of the undead, whose face was covered in green slime. "That's the postman, isn't it?"

Hector nodded. "Yes, the only thing to fear is if you see someone you don't recognise at all. Because then—" he leaned closer for effect "—that means real monsters have risen from the bushes around us. We're not that far from the church graveyard, you know. It's only just over that hill."

I hoped he thought I squealed purely for comic effect.

At that point, the lights dimmed in the other room, and the sound system struck up again with the "Monster Mash" – not a tune to entice Hector to the dance floor. Nor me, either. To be honest, I didn't mind if we sat for a while without dancing, because it gave us the chance to talk to each other away from the restrictions of the shop.

Once the gimmicky songs were out of the way, some lively dance tracks came on, harvested, as Carol had predicted, from decades gone by. I don't know why I was being so traditional and old-fashioned, waiting for Hector to ask me to dance. I should have just grabbed his hand when a song I liked came on and refused to accept no for an answer. As it was, we carried on chatting and drinking till about eleven, when the music started to slow down.

Finally he stood up, set his mask on the bale to save our place, and held out his hand to lead me to the dance floor. I was prickling all over with excitement as we passed through the stable door into the other room, and he deftly swung me into his arms. As we turned around, the Wendlebury Players' float on the far side of the room caught my eye. The chairs had all been borrowed from and returned to the church, but for some unfathomable reason, the chopping blocks on which Ann Boleyn and Catherine Howard had met their execution were still in place, the cardboard axe, now limp with damp, leaning against the backdrop. I hadn't paid much attention to it when I was dancing earlier with Carol, but now I remembered with horror the sight of my first dead body on that float back in August as Ann Boleyn's costume was peeled back to reveal Linda's lifeless scarlet face.

Hector pulled me closer to him so that I could hear what he said over the music. "Are you OK, Sophie?"

"Sorry, yes, I'm – NOOOO!" I stepped back sharply from him and screamed, raising my arm to point in the direction of the Players' float. Emerging from the shadows came the unmistakable figure of the Grim Reaper, sheathed from top to toe in a voluminous black hooded cape concealing his face. He wielded not a cardboard axe but a sharp metal scythe.

The music stopped abruptly and everyone turned to look in the direction that I'd pointed, frozen with horror and confusion. Moving almost in slow motion, the Grim Reaper raised his scythe over the dance floor, pointing it menacingly at every one of us in turn. As the blade glinted beneath the disco lights, there was no doubt that it was potentially a murderous weapon.

Shouts came from the dance floor. "Oi, who the hell is that? Jim? Is it you? That's not funny. Stop arsing about and spoiling things for everyone." Stanley, drawing on his authority as owner of the barn, stepped forward from the back of the hall to challenge the mysterious intruder.

"Not me, mate," called Jim from the doorway, and everyone swivelled round to look at him to make sure. As we turned back to face the trailer, the Grim Reaper darted across the stage to the disco equipment and raised the scythe above his shoulder.

"Look out, love!" shrieked the DJ's wife, and then the barn went dark.

A thundering of steps across the trailer, followed by the slamming of the back door behind it, confirmed the route of the Grim Reaper's escape. In the ensuing pitch black, people fumbled for phones or torches or lighters – whatever they'd brought with them to light their walk down to the barn. The flickering dots of light did nothing to illuminate the culprit, only adding to the eerie atmosphere.

Used to rounding up recalcitrant livestock, Stanley quickly took charge, flashing his penlight torch above his head so we could see where he was. "Quick, boys, after him! Sam, Ted, you go out the back; Trevor, Jim, round the side to the left. Tony, you come with me round the right. Don't let him get away."

Mostly friends since distant boyhood, and therefore not the fastest runners in the room, Stanley and his team stumbled off in search of the prankster. Various younger men, dads of children at the school, followed, some of them pushed into action by their wives. The rest of us turned to each other in horror and puzzlement. Hector hadn't joined the searchers, possibly because I had flung my arms round him and was clinging on to him as if for dear life. Feeling foolish, I let go and gave him a little push.

"Don't let me stop you – go with them if you like."

He held up his mobile phone to look at me by the light of his torch app. "No, it's OK, more than enough have gone in his wake. I'd be miles behind by now. There was no shortage of volunteers."

He aimed his torch at the disco deck. The DJ was kneeling by the severed power cable, shaking his head. Now that the music had stopped, we could hear the generator was still running, but with no connection, it was useless.

"Sorry, folks, there's nothing I can do to fix this now. I'm afraid we'll have to call it a night." He jumped down behind the trailer and switched the generator off.

The dance floor swiftly emptied. Soon a steady trail of villagers was heading disconsolately back up through the slippery fields. Small clusters of people were talking quietly and angrily about the prankster who had spoiled our fun. The rising mist was now shot through with persistent and penetrating rain.

"Thank goodness the kids had gone home," I heard Ella saying to the gorilla a few metres in front of us. "It would have given them nightmares."

And not just the children, I thought.

There was lively speculation as to who the prankster might have been. Perhaps a teenager, or some bored lout with a sick sense of humour who'd come out from Slate Green looking for trouble. No-one except me seemed scared or nervous. They were just cross for having had their evening's fun curtailed.

I had a different theory. "I bet it was the Reverend Neep," I whispered to Hector, seeking his approval before I risked sharing my idea with the crowd.

Hector took off his lion's mask and gave me a quizzical look. "Neep? I hardly think so, Sophie. He may not like Halloween much, but a vicar would never behave like that. He'd get struck off, or whatever they do to disgraced vicars. Defrocked. That's the word I'm looking for."

He let out a little laugh at the very thought. I was glad I hadn't embarrassed myself by suggesting my idea to anyone else, but I wasn't convinced by Hector's swift denial.

Swinging his lion's head by the mane in one hand, and keeping his other arm tightly around me, Hector walked me back to my cottage. He let go of me only to take my key from his pocket and unlock my front door.

"Do you want me to come in?" His voice was gentle.

Of course I did, but by this time not only was I feeling emotionally drained, I was also nauseous from all the wine and dancing, thick with mud at least as far as my knees, wet through from the rain and chilled to the marrow. I didn't want to make the evening any worse by being sick in front of Hector. Nor did I want to seem afraid.

"No, it's OK, thanks. I think I'll call it a night."

"Are you sure you'll be all right on your own?"

I hesitated, about to change my mind until I caught a glimpse of my face in the hallstand mirror. The make-up I'd applied so carefully at the start of the evening had turned into a murky, tear-streaked mess, and my hair looked like I'd been turning cartwheels in a hurricane.

"No, don't worry, I'll be fine. Thanks for walking me home."

Hector let go of the door. "OK, if you're sure. Goodnight, Sophie. See you at work on Monday."

I turned my face away, embarrassed that I looked such a mess. I could have been mistaken for one of the undead we'd been dancing alongside earlier. Hector stepped forward to give me a hug and a paternal kiss on the top of my head. I wasn't sure whether the night had moved our relationship backwards rather than forwards.

He hesitated on the doorstep, his hand still on the door handle. "Bit of a wash-out as a second date, wasn't it?"

At least he still counted it as a date. I tried to be brave.

"Well, not to worry, we've got our meal out next weekend to look forward to."

I stood at the open door just long enough to watch him stride down my front path, close my front gate behind him and rejoin the High Street, where, elegant in his frock coat, he put his lion's mask back on and sauntered off through the mist towards his flat above the bookshop.

22 Gloomy Sunday

When I finally heaved myself out of bed the next morning after a restless night, dreaming of rabid gorillas in wellies running amok with sharpened umbrellas, I could hardly bear to look at the shiny yellow ballgown draped mockingly over the wardrobe door. Beautiful as it was, I wasn't looking forward to donning it again the next day for fear of bringing back the negative associations from the disco. But I knew I'd have to, because Hector and I had promised the children that on Halloween itself, we'd be in fancy dress all day in the shop.

As I made myself some toast and coffee for breakfast, I realised this was the first time since starting work at Hector's House that I'd ever not looked forward to a Monday morning. After all, Monday morning meant seeing Hector after a Sunday without him.

Spreading raspberry jam on my toast, I wondered whether Stanley and his friends had managed to catch the Grim Reaper. A few hundred years ago, they might have lynched him in a place like this. Fancy getting lynched for being the Grim Reaper.

Someone knocked at the kitchen window, and I jumped, sending the jam jar flying off the table. It landed in a blood-red mass of broken glass at my feet. I looked up to see a thin, lined white-haired face peering in at me, a silvery scythe in his hand. It was Joshua, of course.

"I'm sorry if I startled you, my dear," he said, opening the back door to let himself in. I'd fallen into the village habit of leaving it unlocked. "I just thought I'd pop in to see how your party went last night."

"My party?" I looked blank. "Oh, you mean the Halloween Disco. How did you know about that? It was meant to be a secret."

Joshua chuckled. "It's hard to keep secrets in this village, my dear. I trust you enjoyed it."

I nodded dumbly, trying not to stare at the scythe, sparklingly sharp beneath the kitchen spotlights. Surely Joshua could not have been the Grim Reaper? I knew he disapproved of Halloween, but that would be taking it too far. Besides, earlier that evening he'd seemed to have been getting into the spirit of it with the trick-or-treaters in his own benevolent way. Pitching up a few hours later to admonish the whole village for its celebrations seemed an unlikely about-face. Nor did he seem agile enough to escape the middle-aged men who chased after the intruder, never mind the younger ones. Unless his frailty, that had seemed so pronounced lately, was all a clever act to disguise a sinister alter ego. After all, he was still fit enough to keep his garden immaculate.

Joshua followed my gaze to the gleaming blade.

"I don't usually take a scythe to church, you know."

So he'd just got back from church. Now I felt bad for suspecting him. Or was this another bluff? I held my tongue.

"I just happened to find it lying in the churchyard after I'd visited to lay flowers this morning, ready for All Souls' Day. Flowers for Edith – and for May."

I felt even worse for not knowing that this is what you were meant to do on All Souls' Day.

Joshua broke the silence. "It appears Billy left my scythe leaning against the far wall that backs on to the fields above Stanley's barn. I am not best pleased. You should never leave garden tools out overnight, especially in the rain. That's the fastest route to rust."

I frowned. The Grim Reaper couldn't possibly have been Billy. He wasn't tall enough. Besides, he had been propping up the bar all night, dressed as the vicar.

"Why are you blaming Billy?"

Joshua looked at me as if I was the village idiot. "Because Billy uses it to keep the grass down in the churchyard between the graves. He has my scythe on semi-permanent loan. He's meant to keep it safe in the churchyard shed when he's not using it. I knew it was mine the moment I saw it. It was my father's before me, you know." He raised it up and made a few slicing motions through the air. I stood well back. "I recognised the wooden handle, worn smooth from decades of use in his strong hands."

I recognised it too, for different reasons. Joshua stared out of the window absently, and smiled. "My father was born into a different age, my dear. His first job on leaving school at the age of twelve was

139

as a rook scarer. An old fellow who used to farm down yonder took him on to keep the birds off his crops one spring. Then he kept him on to do odd jobs all year round till he was grown into his man's body."

As he patted the scythe's handle affectionately, I noticed how shiny the wood was, and how clean the blade. The culprit had taken care to remove the evidence of last night's escapade. Now the only fingerprints on there would be Joshua's.

Joshua remained preoccupied with his nostalgic reverie. "Of course, I haven't much use for it since they invented the electric mowing machine." He kept his small patch of lawn in immaculate condition with a bright orange hover mower that he must have been nurturing for decades.

I decided to take a risk by telling Joshua about the mysterious apparition at the disco. If he looked less than surprised, I'd have more reason to suspect him. Only half way through did I realise how rash I was being, considering Joshua was listening with a murderous weapon in his hands.

"I don't know who the Grim Reaper was, but it certainly wasn't Billy. There's any number of people it might have been – a teenager or an adult, judging by the height, but the figure was entirely obscured by a big black hood. Lots of men chased after him but I don't know whether they caught him, or where. I'm guessing the culprit must have run up the hill towards the churchyard and dropped the scythe as he climbed over the wall."

I was careful not to mention the vicar, to avoid another lecture about Neep being the best man for the job.

When I'd finished, Joshua stared at the scythe in his hand with the disappointed look of a husband hearing his wife confess to an affair. He seemed far more upset about his scythe than the disco.

"What a disrespectful way to treat a faithful old tool. I wonder whether the vicar can shed any light on the matter. He may have spotted the prankster from his study or bedroom windows, which overlook that part of the churchyard. Still, I'm glad that the practical joker left the scythe in the churchyard, rather than taking it home or tossing it into a hedgerow. I should hate to lose it, especially as it was my father's. And, speaking of my father, will you be joining us for the All Souls' Day service on Wednesday? I think you might find it comforting."

I grimaced.

"Don't look so worried, my dear. It's not a mournful service, more a positive way to remember those who have gone before us, until we meet again."

He'd hit a bullseye on my conscience, but the thought of attending a service led by the Reverend Neep made me feel ill. I struggled to make excuses without offending Joshua.

"Thank you for thinking of me, but I'm not really a churchgoer. I've never been religious. I'd feel like a fish out of water at a church service. I wouldn't know what to do. I used to like singing hymns and Christmas carols at school, and I can recite the

Lord's prayer, but that's about as far as it goes with me."

"Sophie, that doesn't matter. No-one will scold you if you aren't word perfect in the service, or if you have to look at the hymn book to know which words to sing."

I played for time. "When is it again?"

"All Souls' Day, this Wednesday, at 11am."

I spotted an escape route. "Ah, no, you see, I wouldn't be able to get the time off work then. Hector will be away from the shop visiting Slate Green Secondary School's librarian that morning, so I'll be holding the fort." I congratulated myself on my cleverness, knowing that as Joshua would be in church, he would never rumble my lie.

"I'm sure that's an appointment that Hector would willingly change if you asked him."

I fidgeted in my seat. I'm very bad at lying, but that's not the only reason I practically never do it.

Joshua gazed at me thoughtfully as my blush deepened. He eyed the splat of jam on my floor, where it lay, blood red and accusatory, peppered with shattered glass. "Still, don't let me keep you. I see you have some cleaning up to do, and I'm sure you're weary after all your fun last night."

He pushed back his chair, picked up the scythe as if it were a walking stick, and steadied himself with the wooden handle before moving off. "The invitation to the service will remain open, so do come if you change your mind. Good morning to you, my dear."

As I watched him walk unsteadily down my garden path, I wondered whether he knew more than he was letting on about the Grim Reaper. His lecture about the service might just have been a cunning diversion from the subject. If so, his ploy had worked.

Then, to my relief, I remembered Hector's quote from Sherlock Holmes. I was not watching the back of the Grim Reaper from the disco. Joshua's gait was altogether different. This was not the man who escaped, leaping off the trailer and over the churchyard wall.

With a start, I realised I hadn't yet heard how the chase ended.

23 Hung Over

I grabbed my phone to call Hector, ignoring my rule about leaving him in peace on a Sunday. It went straight to voicemail. Then I texted him, and when he didn't reply, I resolved to knock on the door of his flat. Normally it would have felt taboo to disturb him at home on the one day he had off a week, but now that we'd been on two dates, I was prepared to make an exception.

I glanced at the clock. It was nearly noon. I wondered how long it would take him to bleed to death from a scythe wound.

I'd never walked so fast to Hector's House, rehearsing in my head the best way to speak to the emergency services and trying to remember whether or not you were meant to apply pressure to stop open wounds bleeding. To my relief, when I got there, I saw his Land Rover was gone. Unless the Grim Reaper was also a car thief, it at least meant Hector was fit to drive, even if it had been for a trip to hospital.

As I walked back round from the door to his flat to the front of the shop, one of the school mums was passing with her two little boys, each walking a lively Jack Russell. She looked interested to see me there.

"If you're after Hector, he'll have gone to his mum and dad's, I expect. He often goes down to them at Clevedon for Sunday lunch."

There was still so much I didn't know about him.

"Thanks," I said, feeling a little foolish. Given that her children were with her, I didn't like to enquire whether she knew if anyone had been lacerated by the Grim Reaper the night before. As the village shop is closed on Sundays, I decided to head to another excellent source of intelligence and comfort, The Bluebird.

Donald was unhappy. There was hardly any lunchtime trade in the pub, given that a large proportion of the community was still nursing hangovers from the PTA Disco. Being on duty in the pub the night before, he'd missed the excitement of the chase. It was small compensation that once the hunt was called off, most of the men had called into the pub on the pretext of checking whether the Grim Reaper was propping up the bar. Not surprisingly, Donald hadn't served any suspicious strangers dressed in black and bearing a scythe. I supposed there was an outside chance that the Grim Reaper could have been Donald, as we'd not seen him at the disco, but he'd have to have done a very quick change to be serving as usual behind the bar when the thwarted search party arrived.

"So, do you have any theories as to who the prankster might be, Donald?" I tried to sound casual as I stood at the bar, sipping my ginger ale. He'd given me a knowing look when I had ordered a soft drink in preference to my usual wine.

Donald wiped the spotless bar with a cloth, for want of anything better to do. "Not a clue. Whoever it was, he must have been light on his feet. Either that or found a very good hiding place. Though that wouldn't have been hard on such a dark night, especially if he lay low in Stanley's woodland for a while, rather than heading for the churchyard straight away. I'm afraid he's got away scot-free, Sophie." He tucked the cloth into his back pocket. "Still, I suppose no real harm was done. I mean, it's not as if he chopped off anyone's head with his scythe. You all lived to tell the tale, didn't you? It was probably just some teenager, too old to come to the disco as part of the primary school, and too self-conscious to come with his parents." He produced some new beer mats and set a neat pile next to the beer taps. "There's not enough for teens to do in a village like this. They inevitably get into mischief, not thinking of the consequence of their actions. Like that time young Tommy Crowe hid in a wheelie bin on dustbin day till his mum had gone to work so he could bunk off school. Good thing his little sister ratted on him to the bin men, or he'd have been crushed before you could say 'scythe'."

"It didn't feel like innocent mischief to me, Donald," I said. "It felt more like a threat, especially when it was made on the same spot that poor Linda died."

Donald leaned his elbows on the bar.

"I think you're letting your imagination run away with you, Sophie. You know what teenagers are like these days, all Goths and Emos and I don't know what. It doesn't mean anything when they behave like that. When you've known these kids since before they were born, like I have, you know it's just little Sally or Joe or whoever going off on one. I wouldn't lose any sleep over this Grim Reaper lark if I were you. By this time next week, everyone will have forgotten about it and will be on to the next bit of excitement, whatever that may be. There's never a dull moment in Wendlebury, you know."

He gave me such a kindly look that I backed right down. If no-one else was anxious about the whole thing, I shouldn't be either. It would be foolish to share the news that the scythe was Joshua's and risk dragging him into it. And after all, if someone had been killed or even wounded by the Grim Reaper, we'd all know about it by now.

I sat down on a bar stool, watching the bubbles burst in my ginger ale. It wasn't them, it was me. Maybe I just couldn't take a village joke, with my townie ways and silly flights of fancy. It was disappointing, for sure, when I thought I'd become part of the village, but I was completely out of kilter with popular feeling.

Declining Donald's invitation to stay for a pub lunch, I slouched out after just one drink, and glanced up the road to Hector's House to see whether Hector had returned. However his Land Rover was still missing from its parking space at the side of the shop, so I realised I'd have to wait till the next day to find out his take on the matter.

24 The Beast of the Bookshop

After losing myself in *The Adventures of Sherlock Holmes* and a hot bubble bath for most of Sunday afternoon, I challenged myself with cleaning the cottage from top to bottom. By bedtime I realised my spirits had revived a little, as evidenced by the fact that I could think of the word "spirits" without feeling spooked.

On Monday morning, I didn't feel quite as anxious as I'd expected when putting on the Beauty dress to wear in the shop. I hoped Hector hadn't forgotten our plan to wear our costumes all day on Halloween. I'd feel pretty silly if I pitched up in my frock and he was in his usual jeans and t-shirt. After all, it wasn't often that I dressed like the love interest in a fairy tale.

I was in luck. He was once more an exquisitely tailored Beast, and his outfit looked even better in the daylight than in the shadowy barn. He left his mask on the counter all day, which struck me as eerie at first, but by lunchtime I'd got used to it. Hector predicted correctly that any little girls who came into the shop after school would spend ages plaiting and unplaiting its mane.

I just had time before the first customers of the morning arrived to recount my conversations from Sunday with Joshua and Donald. Although everyone kept telling me not to give the incident any further thought, I was glad Hector now also seemed to want to know who had done it. As we tried to narrow down the suspects, I couldn't help but think of us as a team of ace detectives, like Holmes and Watson. I made a mental note of that idea for next year's Halloween costumes, hoping it wouldn't mean I'd have to wear a moustache.

I expounded my deductions so far. "Whoever it was must have known that Joshua had a scythe, and that Billy kept it in the churchyard. Snaffling the scythe and preparing a special costume suggests a premeditated act by someone in the village, not just spur-of-the-moment hijinks by some yob from Slate Green. And it must have been someone agile enough to get away without being caught by the men who chased after him."

Hector toyed thoughtfully with the lace ruffle down the front of his shirt. He seemed to rather like it now he'd got used to wearing it.

"Not necessarily. Stanley and his mates are not famed for their fleetness of foot, and even though some of the younger dads are runners, they'll all have had a bit to drink, which will have reduced their reaction times. Also the rain had made the ground slippery, so they couldn't have run very fast without going base over apex. Besides, the mist had settled at the foot of the valley by that time in the evening, and visibility was poor."

He paused to open a new box of books that had arrived earlier and began to unpack them onto the counter.

"So if the Grim Reaper was stone cold sober and had his escape strategy planned, even the fastest runner won't have stood much chance of catching him after he'd had a head start. But the scythe's identity definitely suggests the culprit is local, or has local knowledge. Maybe we should have a discreet word with Billy about the scythe next time he's in."

To me all the evidence still pointed to the vicar, and I hoped Hector might draw the same conclusion of his own volition.

We were prevented from any further analysis by the arrival of a group of mums back from the first school run after half-term, lightheaded with the relief of being child-free once more. They'd clearly put Saturday night's fiasco behind them and were ready to move on to the next engagement in the village's social calendar.

While I prepared their drinks, they filled me in on the odds for the guy-making competition sweepstake. The shortest odds were still on Jemima, the spirited little girl who had been my first coaching pupil in the village. I wasn't surprised.

"I'd put my money on Jemima any day," I said to her mother. "She's a determined little soul. And I noticed she won first prize in the children's scarecrow-making class at the Village Show, which is basically the same thing."

As I turned to go back to the counter, I forgot I was wearing a long dress and tripped over the skirt, drawing the mums' attention to Carol's handiwork.

"What will you tell the vicar if he comes in and sees you defying his Halloween ban?" one of them asked.

Hector answered for me. "That we're having a storytelling-themed activity day to mark Halloween. That's perfectly reasonable. Most bookshops will be doing something similar today, I'm sure. My shop, my rules - and if he doesn't like them, he can shop elsewhere. I have no problem with that."

"*Grimm's Fairy Tales* ought to be right up his street," said Jemima's mum. "He's like someone who's stepped out of its pages. He'd probably keep children locked up and fatten them for the pot, given the opportunity."

"Better hide that book from the vicar, then," said her friend. "You don't want to give him ideas."

Hector never missed a trick. "Have you ever read the real *Grimm's Fairy Tales*? I've got a super gift edition tucked away on a shelf somewhere in the children's fiction section."

I hoped his quick wittedness might yet help me get to the bottom of the mystery of the Grim Reaper.

25 Penny for the Billy

Late afternoon I had a different fright on my way back from posting parcels at the post office.

As I passed the pub, I noticed a dark figure slumped on the pavement in front of Hector's House, amidst a pile of dead sycamore leaves from next door's front garden. I was sure it hadn't been there when I'd left the shop half an hour before. As it was starting to get dark already, I couldn't make out who it was without getting closer.

I broke into a run, lifting my gown in both hands to save me falling headlong on the way. Skidding to a halt outside the bookshop, I shouted for Hector and banged on the shop window to get his attention. Then I stooped to tend to the figure, whose face was concealed beneath a wide-brimmed black felt hat. Its body wrapped in a brown overcoat that covered the tops of riding boots, it lay entirely motionless.

Had the Grim Reaper struck again?

I reached for one limp wrist to find a pulse and shrieked when it suddenly sprang to life and grabbed me back with a vice-like grip. I found myself being shouted at for my trouble.

"Oi, what do you think you're playing at, girlie? You're too late to ask me to dance."

With its free hand, the figure lifted its hat to reveal Billy's familiar face.

Hector emerged from the shop, looking even more dashing in his Beast costume next to Billy's ragged outfit.

"What on earth—?" Hector bent down to pick up a battered flat cap that lay on the pavement the other side of Billy and fished out a couple of sodden brown leaves, a twenty-pence piece and an old Manila envelope, on the back of which was written in wobbly pencil: "Penny for the Guy".

"You're five days early, Billy. Or rather, about forty years too late, because that's how long it is since anyone last went begging for a Penny for the Guy in this village. It's not as if you even bothered to make a proper guy. It's just you in old clothes. Sitting still and looking scruffy doesn't make you a guy, you know. Now get up and stop cluttering up my shopfront."

Billy groaned as he staggered to his feet. "Well, I call that downright ungrateful, young Hector. I picked that spot very carefully. I thought if the vicar came by, he'd think you'd had a change of heart and was doing things his way. I'm showing the kiddies how Penny for the Guy is done. And I'm being scary for Halloween at the same time. So I'm giving them the best of both worlds and providing you with an extra attraction for your shop. It'll make people stop and look at Hector's House."

"Make people cross the street to avoid it, you mean." Hector scowled. "Penny for the Guy indeed. Penny for the beer, more likely. How much beer will Donald let you have for twenty pence?"

Grumbling, Billy snatched the flat cap and its contents back from Hector, stuffed it in his coat pocket, and turned to trudge off home.

As Hector held the door open for me to go back into the bookshop, I realised I was trembling. To my embarrassment, as soon as I got inside, I burst into tears.

"Sophie, what's wrong?"

I fell into his outstretched arms, too distressed to enjoy his embrace as much as I should have done.

"I'm sorry, Hector. For a few minutes, I was convinced it was a dead body. I assumed one of our customers had been struck down by the Grim Reaper as punishment for our transgressions against the vicar's will."

I felt Hector tense. "What on earth do you mean? You're not taking Neep's threats seriously, are you? He doesn't really have any power over us. The man's just a bully. And anyway, the Grim Reaper at the disco wasn't a murderer, just some silly prankster. He didn't kill anyone – just pulled the plug on the disco."

"Hacked at a cable with a lethal weapon, you mean."

"Pah! The only person at any real risk at the disco was the prankster himself. He's lucky he didn't get electrocuted, slicing through a live wire with a blade. He must have been wearing wellington boots beneath his robe, so he wasn't earthed, which is just as well."

He gave a flicker of a smile. "Or, of course, he could have been a her." Now he was just trying to wind me up. I pulled myself away, feeling foolish and embarrassed, and went to sit on the furthest tearoom chair. Turning my back to him to wipe my eyes with a serviette, I realised from the dark marks that appeared on the white paper that my mascara must be badly smudged.

"I thought it might have been you, Hector."

When he looked offended rather than flattered, I realised Billy didn't look at bit like Hector really. I tried again. "Or a vision of something terrible to come."

Then I decided to get straight to the point. I'd had enough of playing games.

"You know, the more I think about it, the more I am convinced that the vicar was the Grim Reaper. I mean, I can't believe it wasn't him. Isn't it obvious?"

Hector pulled a chair up close to mine and sat down, his hands on my knees. As he leaned forward, I couldn't help but notice the neat curve of his velvet costume breeches stretching taut across his thighs.

"Sophie, I think you're letting your feelings run away with you. That whole business on Saturday night was just a village prank in dubious taste. Not one of Wendlebury's better jokes, and best forgotten. I mean, I know I'm not exactly Neep's best friend, but even I don't think a clergyman would do something so crass."

"But Reverend Murray did. Joshua told me he dressed up last Halloween as the Pope, and his wife went as Mother Teresa."

Hector chuckled at the memory. "Yes, but that was good-natured. It's not like they spent the evening waving sharp knives around. No, Mr Neep might not like Halloween, but as a vicar he will be a responsible adult, not a madman. Trust me, the Grim Reaper will turn out to be some hormonal, moody teenager. We've got a few of those tucked away in Wendlebury who emerge from their bedrooms to play ill-conceived practical jokes now and again. Like when Tommy Crowe put on a false beard and tried to convince Donald he was a beer inspector from the brewery. And Billy told me once that Tommy had asked to borrow his scythe for the weekend. That boy's too interested in sharp instruments for his own good. My money's on Tommy. But he's harmless, really."

I sniffed, rubbing my eyes "OK, don't believe me then."

"But what is there to believe?"

"My instincts. I'm following my instincts. I'm not completely stupid, you know." I didn't want to be snapping at Hector, but I couldn't help it. This should have been a lovely day, with us flitting about gracefully in our beautiful costumes, looking like the perfect couple. Instead it was turning sour.

I tried again. "And what about what the vicar said about Halloween?"

The shop door creaked open behind us.

"Speaking of which—" Hector, facing the door, saw the visitor before I did. I swivelled round to see Mr Neep had planted himself by the till, hovering in his usual sombre suit and his black shoes. I felt like I'd summoned him up.

Hector stood his ground, waiting to judge the tenor of his visit.

157

"Ah, Mr Hector." I allowed myself the slightest of smiles at Neep's opening gambit. How could a vicar be so bad at getting the names of his parishioners right? I wouldn't put it past him to forget his own.

"How can I help you, vicar?"

I was glad to see Hector smiling politely, prepared as ever to be the bigger person.

The vicar stepped forward and gave a strained attempt at a smile, holding out a couple of sheets of paper and purposely averting his gaze from Hector's flamboyant costume. His eyes never dropped below Hector's chin. "I am distributing further intelligence about two important events in this week's village calendar. The All Souls' Day service on Wednesday and the Guy Fawkes party on Saturday. You might make amends for your clear flouting of my advice about Halloween by displaying them in your shop window in the intervening passage of time."

The vicar avoided eye contact with either of us, and I felt he was holding something back.

Hector read the posters in silence, keeping the vicar on tenterhooks. "I suppose I could accomplish that conciliatory request." I don't know how he kept a straight face as he mimicked the vicar's convoluted manner of speaking.

From beneath the counter he pulled a tub of drawing pins and proceeded to add the posters to the corkboard beside the shop door. "This is where we customarily display public notices, so as not to obstruct our customers' inspection of our windowly display."

Hector was on a roll.

"As the proprietor of this emporium, it is my pleasure to support local eventualities here via the instruments of advertising." He returned to his seat behind the counter, and leaned forward to fix the vicar with a knowing look. "We *reap* what we sow in this village. Perhaps you may care to reciprocate when we are holding in-store events ourselves? Too late of course to promote our *Grimm*'s Fairy Tales day today."

I clapped my hand over my mouth to stop myself laughing out loud at Hector's clever word games. It was sweet of him to try to allay my fears and cheer me up like this.

"Though that particular purveyor of tales was *Grimm* by name, he wasn't always *Grimm* by nature. Admittedly some of the stories are rather dark, and there's too much *chasing about in the night* for my taste, but good always seems to triumph over evil. At least in the Disney versions."

The vicar backed towards the door, looking perplexed. "Another time, perhaps, Mr House." He reached behind him for the door handle, whisked it open, and let it slam behind him in his haste to escape.

Hector let out a bark of laughter and strode back triumphant to the tearoom. He pulled out a chair, turned it round to face away from the table, and sat astride it back to front in an uncharacteristic display of machismo.

"I must confess I enjoyed that a little more than I should have done. I might have to go to his wretched party after all to salve my conscience for

159

being mean to a customer. But at least it's made you smile, so that's something."

"Thank you, Hector. Although you do realise that if he wasn't the Grim Reaper, he'll think you're completely mad now? Oh my goodness!" A horrible thought struck me. "He could have come to the disco as a Beast like you and got away with it. It was – it was you that walked me home, wasn't it?"

"So have you forgotten the moments when I took my mask off to talk to you – and to kiss you? I must be losing my touch." Hector laughed. "I hope you'd be able to tell us apart, even in full costume. If I pitched up in a vicar outfit tomorrow, would you mistake me for Mr Neep?"

He had a point. Though they were of similar height, they had completely different builds. Neep was wiry and thin, whereas Hector had just the right amount of muscle.

"Funny how he seemed so nervous, though," I said. "Do you think our costumes put him off?"

Hector shook his head. "No, he probably just didn't like having to ask us a favour, after swearing he'd have nothing to do with the shop." He looked down at the posters. "Honestly, you'd think a grown man could do a better job of publicity than this. I'm guessing he's worried that not many people will show up."

Hector's words about reaping what you sow were echoing in my head, and I tried to be as kind to Neep as I'd like him to be to me. "Perhaps he's just very shy. Maybe he'll be more confident on his own territory, like the vicarage and in church."

"My goodness, you're being very charitable, Sophie."

I shrugged. "I'm thinking a priest is used to being the centre of attention, unchallenged by his audience, and to having the feeling of being right, what with having his god on his side." I toyed with the spoon in the sugar bowl, scooping up the crystals and letting them rain slowly down again into the dish.

Hector reached across the table to still my hands. "Let's hope he's not so confident at his party that he gets carried away and starts burning witches at the stake. Better warn whoever was dressed as a witch on Saturday to stay away."

I gasped, freed my hands, and knocked over the sugar bowl. "Surely not?"

"Sophie, I'm joking. Though if he were to choose a victim, I bet I'd be on his hit list. And Billy."

I rounded up the spilled sugar grains with the side of my hand and brushed them back into the bowl. Hector leaned back and stretched wearily.

"I doubt he's got the courage to go breaking the law, to be honest. For all his bluster, he strikes me as fundamentally weak, but I could be wrong."

I emitted a sigh of defeat.

"You and Donald are probably right. The Grim Reaper was more likely a bored teenager. Whoever it was will be rumbled soon enough because they won't be able to keep the secret to themselves and will start boasting about it. This morning it will have been the talk of the bus that the older kids catch to secondary school."

Hector thought for a moment, running through the eligible bored teenagers in his head. "The more I think about it, the more I am sure it was Tommy Crowe. He's a tall, lanky kid, with the right kind of build, and an unresolved grudge against the world. Poor kid was abandoned by his dad when he was a toddler, and his mum's been nurturing his sense of resentment against the world ever since. He's usually behind most village mischief that doesn't originate in the pub. Apart from the wife-swapping, of course."

"What?"

"Joke." Hector was straight-faced, but nothing would surprise me in Wendlebury Barrow.

I picked my moment. "Speaking of losing people, do you think I could duck out of the shop for an hour on Wednesday morning to go to the All Souls' service?"

Hector looked surprised. "I didn't think you were religious."

"No, I'm not, but Joshua was pretty persuasive yesterday that I ought to go. And to be honest, if I didn't go, I'd feel I was letting him and Auntie May down. I still feel bad for missing her funeral."

Hector knew I'd been working in Germany at the time and was unable to get away.

"Yes, that was a shame. It was a wonderful celebration. Standing room only, hymns and readings from her favourite travel destinations. Highly cosmopolitan by Wendlebury Barrow's standards." He reached for my hands again, in tenderness this time rather than to stop me vandalising condiments. "Cinders, you shall go to

162

the service. But first, please chuck that sugar away now that it's been all over the table. You don't want to add further mayhem by giving our tearoom customers food poisoning."

I smiled weakly. "Thank you, Buttons."

26 All Souls' Surprise

On the Wednesday morning, I donned subdued colours ready for church. Although May's gorgeous black silk cardigan would have been perfect, I didn't want to risk looking more like her than my genes dictated, for fear of upsetting Joshua. I also left off my make-up to guard against panda eyes.

I was glad to be going to work for the first couple of hours of the morning so I didn't build myself up into a high state of emotion before crossing the church threshold. I hoped an emergency at the bookshop might detain me at the last minute.

"I don't have to go if you can't spare me." The place was empty apart from Hector as I cleared the cups and plates after the morning school run. "It's not like it's her funeral. I'm sure there'll be another All Souls' service next year and every year after that."

"Yes, and you could visit May's grave any day you wanted to in the meantime."

He'd caught me there. I was starting to find Hector's knowledge of me unnerving. I'd only once visited May's grave in the churchyard since my arrival when I'd been shocked to discover it was just a rough mound of dirt, marked by a small wooden cross. It hadn't occurred to me that a neat

165

gravestone and flower bed wouldn't already be in place. The experience had made May's loss seem raw and new.

When I'd phoned my parents in tears afterwards, my dad explained that you can't install a gravestone for at least six months after a burial, because the ground must settle first, otherwise the stone will just keel over. He'd ordered a suitable headstone to be installed in the new year. I took that as permission to postpone further visits till then.

I seized the dishcloth from the sink and wiped the tearoom tables for longer than necessary. "You think I should go, don't you?"

Hector put down the last of the new novels he'd been arranging on the display table and came over to the tearoom. He pulled out a chair and beckoned me to it, then seated himself opposite.

"To be honest, yes, I do. I think it would help you. You've got a bit of unresolved grief going on, and it's one constructive thing you can do to help that's easily within your reach."

I stretched my arms across the table as if in surrender, forgetting it would still be damp. My grey shirt sleeves turned black with the moisture.

"But how can you say that when you're not a churchgoer either? It's not as if you're the vicar's number one fan."

Hector took my hands and held them gently. "No, I'm just thinking of you. And besides, it would make Joshua happy. Poor old soul, he's rooting for two down there, both Edith and May, and could doubtless do with your moral support."

I pulled one hand free to jab him in the chest. "You are right, of course. I feel like I owe it to Joshua. He's been a good friend to me. But if I go, I won't be responsible for my state of mind on my return to the shop."

Hector winked. "I didn't know you ever were."

Even though I had now resolved to go to the service, I left it till the very last minute to head to the church. Through the shop window, I watched several likely candidates for the congregation walk past, heads bowed in contemplation. When I saw Joshua, I expected him to turn and raise his hat to me, as he usually did. But he appeared lost in his memories of the two great loves of his life. He must also have been thinking of his parents, and all his other relations and friends who had been laid to rest in St Bride's churchyard. This was not all about me.

Slipping into my dark winter coat a couple of minutes before eleven, I gave Hector a little wave as I left, and he gave me an encouraging thumbs-up sign. As I dawdled towards the church, I found myself reliving precious memories with Auntie May as if I'd been given permission not to grieve but to celebrate. As I turned into the church porch, I realised I was smiling.

The heavy oak door was closed. I glanced at my watch to discover it was a few minutes after the hour already, so I heaved the door ajar as slowly and as quietly as I could, just wide enough for me to squeeze through before pulling it shut behind me. I was committed now.

Tiptoeing into the nearest pew, right at the back of the church, I picked up a service sheet from the seat, opened it and held it up in front of me, peering from behind it like a spy with a newspaper to see who else was there.

Scattered at random on the shiny dark pews were a couple of dozen people, many of whom I recognised from around the village, such as Joshua, Donald and his wife, and Trevor and Tilly. I hoped Carol hadn't just come for an opportunity to get closer to Mr Neep, then I admonished myself for such an unworthy thought. Of course, she'd come for her late parents.

Joshua's advice to give Mr Neep a chance returned to me. I had come to realise over the last few months how wise and dignified my neighbour was. Although my generation might have all the facts (and fictions) of the internet at our fingertips, we don't trump the accumulated life experience of an intelligent and considerate old soul in his ninth decade who has never read an email in his life.

I'd missed the opening address, and the vicar was now instructing the congregation to rise for the first hymn. I stared at the lyrics on the service sheet, which were set to a tune I didn't recognise, and mimed as convincingly as I could so as not to seem out of place. To my surprise, as everyone sang out, I found the hymn unexpectedly moving and comforting. Warmth emanated from the friends around me as together we raised our voices for our lost loved ones. By the third verse, I had mastered the tune and found myself singing with full voice and gusto, though tears spilled freely down my cheeks. I wondered how many times May had sung these words, taking part in this ceremony as she remembered those she too had lost in her long life. For a moment, I felt the soft touch of her hand upon mine.

As the final chords from the organ reverberated around the church, I surreptitiously wiped my face dry and, taking my cue from what everyone else did, sat down again. Returning to the role of watcher rather than participant, I became transfixed by the vicar. It was the first time I'd seen him in his comfort zone, and I realised that much of his awkward manner had disappeared. It was as if he was on autopilot. It was also the first time I'd seen him in his full vicar's regalia rather than a suit and dog collar. Now he wore a long violet robe over a black one which swung pleasingly as he turned. It would have been great for dancing. I tried to imagine what his dancing style might be like – dad dancing, presumably.

I looked away, conscious that I was staring, and hoping Mr Neep wouldn't notice me and catch my eye. Fortunately he had his head buried in the prayer book now, which surprised me. For a vicar of his age, I thought he would have known the service off by heart, the number of times he must have conducted it.

Then, as he lowered the book and turned his back to the congregation to progress towards the altar, my attention was galvanised. I recognised that rangy walk; those long, loping strides; that slightly lopsided angle of the shoulders on a leftward lean; the swing of his thin, gangly arms.

I clapped my hands over my mouth for fear of what I might shout out, then sidled as quietly as I could out of the pew. The congregation was too intent on the vicar's words to notice my escape.

I charged up the High Street and hurled myself back into the safety of Hector's House and leant against the closed door behind me to catch enough breath to speak.

"I've just seen the Grim Reaper in church."

Hector was on the phone, but fortunately the shop was free of customers. He quickly finished his call and replaced the handset.

"Well, I suppose he would have a lot of people to mourn."

I slid out of my coat and hung it on the hook behind the counter. "You know what Sherlock Holmes says about backs? I recognised his back as he walked up the aisle in his long black dress. He may not have been wearing the hooded cape that he used on Saturday, but I'm certain."

I crossed the shop to slump onto one of the tearoom chairs, my heart still pounding, and not just from my sprint. "I would stake my life on Mr Neep being the Grim Reaper."

Hector's smile disappeared. "Let's hope it doesn't come to that." Joining me in the tearoom, he flicked down the switch on the electric kettle and fetched the special cream for a spot of medicinal tea. "But why on earth would a vicar do something like that? He may not approve of Halloween, but that's hardly professional or orthodox behaviour."

I considered. "Perhaps he's just deranged."

Hector pulled out the chair opposite me and sat down. "No, or the diocese wouldn't have appointed him. I know it's not easy to find priests for rural parishes, but they're not that desperate. And to be fair, you still don't have any proof that it was him, nor much of a motive, beyond his disapproval of Halloween. That kind of reaction would be a bit over the top."

"There was Joshua's scythe in his churchyard."

"Yes, but anyone could have borrowed Joshua's scythe and left it in the churchyard. It's a public place. It's not as if you found it in the vicar's study." He drummed his fingers on the table top. "You know, I'm not sure this gets us much further unless he gets up to any more tricks. And I'm not sure what we'd be accusing him of, beyond a tasteless practical joke and wilful damage to an electrical cable. I'm sorry, Sophie, but I think it's now just a question of 'Watch and wait', as medics like to say, to see what happens next."

27 Old Tricks for New Vicar

Having got the service out of the way, the vicar reverted to his favourite hobby of seeking out sin in the village. Tommy Crowe was the current focus of his wrath.

Ella called me after work to report on Mr Neep's visit to the school that afternoon. "Apparently a gang of older kids turned up at the vicarage late on Monday night in fancy dress to try their luck trick-or-treating. They were old enough to be out on their own, rather than with their parents, and some of them were as tall as the vicar himself."

I settled myself down on the sofa. "Why did he complain to you about them? Surely he must have realised they were too old to be your pupils?"

"He claims it's our fault for not shaping their moral fortitude when they were with us in their formative years."

"On that basis, he could blame you for almost everything that goes wrong in the village," I said, swinging my feet up onto the coffee table.

"Honestly, Sophie, what's the vicar's problem? If he didn't want trick-or-treaters, all he had to do was turn them away empty-handed. But instead he gave them such an earful that after he'd gone back inside,

173

they decided to resort to tricks and let his car tyres down." *

I knew I shouldn't laugh, but I couldn't help it. "So how did you resolve his complaint?"

"I told him there was nothing I could do about it. But the stupid thing is, I felt guilty, even though it had nothing to do with the school. He has a real knack for making people feel bad about themselves. I'm just glad he didn't seem to know about the disco."

I decided not to tell her I thought the vicar had been at the disco in disguise. As Ella's friend, I wanted to soothe her rather than add to her stress. I was glad to hear she had been assertive in the face of his accusations.

"After he'd gone, I put a call in to Tommy's mum. As you can imagine, I got to know her quite well in the school office before he went up to secondary school. We called her in to see the Head whenever he was particularly badly behaved. She always said she'd talk to him about his pranks, but she never did."

I heard Ella pause to swig from a drink which I suspected was a post-school glass of wine. "So this time I decided to be a bit more creative, and suggested that he might make it up to the vicar by doing something to support his Bonfire Night party, such as making a decent guy or collecting firewood for the bonfire." I heard the sound of liquid pouring as she topped up her glass. "Even if it wasn't him who let the vicar's tyres down, he's less trouble when he has a project on the go. He'd make a good job of it, too. He never does anything by halves. He's either going to end up in prison or become Prime Minister, or possibly both."

"Well done, Ella, it sounds like you were the perfect diplomat. I don't see what more you could have done. I think Neep's lucky you heard him out. Maybe talking about it will have made him feel better. So did you part with him on good terms or is he still blaming the school?"

"He was surprisingly conciliatory, pressing me as to whether I'd be going to his wretched Guy Fawkes party. Before the end of the day, he'd brought me in a flyer to photocopy for the kids' book bags, encouraging them to enter the guy competition and come along to burn them at his party. If that doesn't lead to an outbreak of pyromania in the village, I don't know what will."

"It's a good thing Carol keeps the matches well out of the reach of kids," I said.

"But Tommy's in the Scouts," said Ella. "If he wants to set light to the vicarage, he'll know how to rub two sticks together. But don't tell anyone I said that. I don't want to give Tommy ideas."

Nor anyone else, I thought.

28 Penance by Proxy

I'd hardly put the phone down when there was an insistent rapping at the door. Not expecting anyone, I peered through the small window. I didn't think it'd be a call from the Grim Reaper, but nor did I recognise the face staring back at me, nose pressed against the glass. It was a tall boy in his early teens, the odd bristle of facial hair erupting from an otherwise girlish complexion. Narrow cat-like grey eyes met mine, with the self-assurance of one who felt he had a right to peer uninvited into other people's homes. But he looked harmless enough, and hardly more than a child, despite his height, so I opened the door, my curiosity aroused.

The scrawny boy stepped forward as if I'd invited him in. I very much had not. Planting my feet firmly on the threshold, I held the door with one hand, in case of an urgent need to slam it against him, and braced myself with the other hand against the door jamb.

"Hello, I'm Tommy Crowe," he said brightly, as if that explained everything. "I know who you are."

After my conversation with Ella, I had a pretty good idea of what he'd come about. "Hello, Tommy Crowe. What can I do for you?" As I said it, I wondered at this boy's power to make me immediately put myself at his disposal. I've always envied the type of person who can ask you to do something and make you feel that they've done you a favour.

"I'm collecting firewood for the new vicar. Have you got any I could have, please?" He gestured to a huge empty wheelbarrow that he'd left blocking my front gate, then leaned forward to peer pointedly behind me at the wood-burner in the front room. I tensed my arm against the door jamb.

"Yes, I have firewood, but I also have a wood-burning stove. Hence the firewood. I need it. It's for me, not for you, and not for the vicar either."

Tommy creased his smooth young brow. "That's what everybody's saying. Honestly, I don't see why you all have to be so selfish about it. The Bonfire Party's for the whole village."

He looked so genuinely perplexed that I nearly weakened. "Well, it is November, Tommy, and that's just the time of year when people start lighting their wood-burners of an evening. If you were to ask in midsummer, you might get a better response."

I didn't like to confess that I hadn't yet mastered the art of lighting my stove and keeping it going. I bet he could have given me a lesson in fire-lighting, had I asked him.

Tommy looked disconsolately at the doorstep. "Yes, but I can't wait till then, can I? The vicar needs it for Saturday. It's no good telling everyone they'll have to wait till summer for Guy Fawkes' Night."

I couldn't dispute his logic. Considering Tommy had just let Mr Neep's tyres down, or maybe because of that, I felt more sympathetic to the boy than I should have done. I was also glad I didn't have a car myself that might attract his attention if I sent him away empty-handed.

Thinking of the vicar helped me harden my heart. "It's down to the vicar to organise his own wood. It's his party, after all."

Tommy pondered for a moment, then pointed to the hallstand behind me. "What about those walking sticks?" In the umbrella rack stood a few of my aunt's souvenirs from her hiking trips, carved forest wood from various destinations in eastern Europe and North America. "You're hardly going to fit those in your wood-burner, are you? And you don't need them, because you haven't got a limp." He looked appraisingly at my legs, taking rather longer than I felt comfortable with. Perhaps he wasn't such a child after all. "Why don't you donate those?"

Clever phrasing, young Tommy, I noticed, using the word "donate" to imply I'd be helping a charity.

"Well, for one thing, they're valuable artefacts, and if I did decide to use them as firewood, I could easily cut them into small enough pieces to fit into my wood-burner."

I didn't mention that I hadn't yet mastered the axe in the woodshed either.

"That's two things, and I don't know what farty acts are."

I bet you do, I thought.

Then he brightened. "But if you need wood chopped, just ask me. I'm very handy with an axe. I chop all the wood for my mum."

179

Something told me I shouldn't let this man-boy loose in my house with an axe. Then I saw my chance to get the upper hand at last.

"So has your mum donated firewood for the vicar's bonfire?"

Tommy looked as if I'd asked him whether she could fly. "Oh God, no. She says he ought to make his own bonfire." He narrowed his eyes even further. "She's a lot like you, you know."

I wasn't sure whether this was an insult or a compliment, but took heart from Ella's tip-off that he was devoted to his mother.

"My mum said if I wanted to help Mr Neep, I ought to make a guy to burn instead. I thought collecting wood would be easier. I guess I was wrong."

I made a mental note to ask Hector to point out Tommy's mum to me if she ever came into the shop. I'd be interested in seeing what she was like.

"So make a guy. Problem solved."

Tommy looked at his feet, for the first time abashed. "I don't know how to make a guy. And besides, I haven't got any clothes to make one out of. I need a man's clothes. My dad left us when I was three, and my mum burnt all his clothes then."

That melted my resistance. Out of the corner of my eye, I noticed Joshua drawing his front room curtains, nodding to me and Tommy in greeting as he did so. That gave me an idea.

"I tell you what, why don't you ask Joshua to help you? He's been telling me how much he enjoyed making guys when he was a boy, so he'll be an expert. He might even find some old clothes of his own to start you off, if you ask him nicely."

Tommy's mood brightened immediately, and I was pleased for him, guessing no father figure had stepped in to fill his void. I was glad for Joshua, too, who probably wouldn't have bothered to make a guy on his own but might love to be the catalyst for the youngest generation to carry on his boyhood tradition.

"You don't think he'd mind?"

"I think he'd be glad you asked him."

I hoped I wasn't overestimating Joshua's generosity, but having seen how popular he was among the children at Hector's House, and how much he thrived on their company, I thought it was worth a try. He always seemed to walk more easily when leaving the shop after chatting with the children, as if he'd absorbed a dose of their youth and energy. In any case, Joshua would have known Tommy since he was a baby, and Tommy's father too, so it's not as if I was inflicting a stranger on him.

"I'll do it." With animal grace, Tommy leaped over the low lavender hedge that divided my front path from Joshua's to save himself the bother of navigating around the wheelbarrow he'd left at my gate. Landing as neatly as a cat, he knocked tentatively on Joshua's door.

A qualm of guilt spreading over me, I stayed where I was, waiting to hear the old man's familiar slow footfall. As Joshua opened the door, I smiled encouragingly at Tommy.

"Good evening to you, young scallywag." It sounded as if no introduction was needed, but I thought it best to ease the way.

"Hello, Joshua, I hope you don't mind, but Tommy's after some expert advice on how to make a guy. I told him you were the best person in Wendlebury to talk to about that."

Joshua looked gratified. "I'd be glad to, and glad of your company this dark evening, Master Crowe. Don't expect me to do the work for you, but I'll point you in the right direction. You can start by threading a needle for me. Threading needles needs young eyes."

I felt sure they'd make a great team. Just before Tommy skipped over the doorstep to follow Joshua inside, he turned to me with a wide-eyed smile.

"Thanks, miss. You're a good person."

Unsure why an awkward compliment from a reprobate should give me such a warm glow, I closed my front door and left them to their complicity, hoping I'd done the right thing. Only afterwards did it occur to me that I'd given Tommy another reason to play with fire. I was just glad I hadn't given him the sticks with which to start one.

29 The Mysterious Guy

Next day, Hector really did have an appointment at Slate Green Comprehensive School. He was due to see the librarian and the head of English at the end of the school day. This meant I was in charge of the shop for an hour, which always made me slightly nervous, even though I enjoyed pretending I was the proprietor.

As I cleared the tea things after the end-of-school rush, I was just musing to myself what I'd call my own bookshop, dithering between Sayers' Pages and Sophie's Choice Books, when a stranger arrived. I put him in his early thirties. In his shiny and ill-fitting business suit and plain dark tie, he looked out of place in our village and in Hector's House. We didn't get many customers in suits that weren't tweed. His sturdy black shoes shone almost as much as his suit, his startling lime green socks providing a clear marker where his feet ended and his legs began.

I thought he might be lost on his way to a business meeting. If so, I could sell him a road atlas, unless he had satnav. I was always pleased when I made sales in Hector's absence, dropping them into conversation casually on his return, as proof of my value to the shop's viability.

The stranger's opening gambit, therefore, took me by surprise. "Do you by any chance stock *My Life in a Sentence* by Septimus Vance?"

I couldn't resist the obvious quip. "That can't be a very long book."

The stranger sighed. I suspect he'd heard that joke before. "But do you stock it? It would be in your memoir section."

"I'm afraid we don't. But if you know the ISBN, I could order it, and we could probably have it in the shop for you to collect by the end of tomorrow. There's no charge for ordering, but we do ask you to pay in advance."

The stranger put up his hand to stop me. "Oh no, I don't want another copy, thanks. I just wondered whether you stocked it. I heard the author had moved to the area recently and I was curious as to whether he might have left you some copies to sell. If he had, I thought you might be able to give me his phone number."

I shook my head. "Sorry, can't help you on that one. I've not heard of him, I'm afraid. But we wouldn't give out our customers' private information to strangers anyway. You must have heard of the Data Protection Act." I suddenly clicked that he might be some kind of mystery shopper for our distributors, trying to test our customer service. No wonder he was laying it on a bit thick.

I tried a different tack. "Well, do you have an AI sheet about it?"

He looked blank.

"You know, an advance information sheet – the sheets you publishers' reps give to booksellers?" I realised he must be a new recruit, which was why we'd never seen him before. I'd enjoyed getting to know the reps that called on us regularly to pitch their authors' new books. They were usually cheerful, upbeat, outgoing characters, but this one seemed strangely edgy. I didn't hold out much hope for his chances of meeting his sales quota, the way he was going. "I'm not saying we would stock it, unless it's a good fit for our customers, but as you're here, I can run your AI sheet past my boss when he gets back."

Shaking his head, the rep turned away, probably embarrassed at his ineptitude, and gazed around the shop as if hoping to find Septimus Vance himself on a display table. Then he turned back to me, realising I'd rumbled him.

"OK, no worries, then." He seemed remarkably defeatist for a salesman. "I only stopped by to ask directions to the vicarage. I'm meeting a friend there."

Not knowing the vicar, he didn't realise what an unlikely cover story that was. I couldn't believe that Mr Neep might have a friend. He no more knew how to be sociable than to turn invisible, but perhaps I was being too harsh. Perhaps it just took a while to get to know him.

Making one last stab at being helpful, I led the rep out of the shop to point him in the right direction.

"It's the last house on the right at the end of the village, set back a bit from the road, with a big holly hedge along the front. You can't miss it."

With no further comment, he ambled away, and I was glad to return to the warmth of the shop. I'd just sat down on Hector's stool behind the counter, planning out of curiosity to look up *My Life in a Sentence* on our supplier's database, when the shop's landline rang.

Before I could even say "Hello", Carol's voice, breathless with anxiety, blurted out, "Tommy Crowe's pushing Joshua in a wheelbarrow."

I stared into the handset in astonishment. "What, you mean Joshua is standing next to a wheelbarrow and Tommy's pushing him into it?"

"No, no, Joshua's just lying in it, helpless, arms and legs dangling all over the place. He's probably unconscionable. Or dead. And Tommy's pushing the wheelbarrow, dead body and all, up the High Street."

"Well, why didn't you stop him?"

"I didn't see him. Old Mrs Mason on the corner phoned me while I was in the stockroom to tell me that he'd just passed hers, but by the time I'd got back to the counter, I'd missed him. So he's probably just about to reach Hector's House now. Quick, go out and stop him before it's too late."

"I can't leave the shop unattended. Hector's out." I glanced across to the shop window just in time to see the back end of Tommy Crowe, wheelbarrow handles in his hands, disappear in the direction of the school. "I know, I'll phone Ella Berry. She's probably still in the school office and might be able to leap out and stop him in his tracks with a citizen's arrest."

I pressed the "call end" button and then the school's speed dial code, while running to the door and flinging it open, almost knocking the returning Hector off his feet. As soon as Ella picked up, I shouted, "Quick, Ella, run out to the front of the school and look down the street. Tommy Crowe's heading your way with a dead body in a wheelbarrow."

Ella sounded bemused. "But I don't want a dead body in a wheelbarrow."

Hector, by contrast, went into overdrive. "Sophie, stay here, and call the police. And an ambulance, in case it's not too late." He started to run up the High Street towards the school.

"What about our village bobby?" I said, before remembering that, mid-afternoon, Bob would be on duty at the Slate Green police station. I grabbed my mobile phone and dialled 999 as I followed Hector up the High Street, garbling a breathless description of events to the emergency switchboard operator. He told me to stay on the line till the services arrived, in case reinforcements were needed.

Hector sprinted until he reached the school's front boundary wall, where he caught up with Tommy, who was casually pushing his wheelbarrow along with no idea of the turmoil he'd caused. Hector firmly clamped one hand on the boy's shoulder, as if apprehending a shoplifter. Tommy's indignant "Oi!" carried all the way down the High Street, but was quickly silenced by a downpour of dry sand. Ella, seizing the first defensive weapon that

187

had come to hand, had emptied the contents of a school fire bucket over Tommy and Hector's heads.

"It was the closest thing I had to a pepper spray," Ella was saying as I caught up with them. Hector and Tommy shook sand from their hair like Labradors drying themselves after a swim in the village pond.

Tommy eyed the fire bucket accusingly. "It's not like my guy's on fire already. Not till Saturday night. And I don't think you should go putting out fires then either, not unless you want to spoil the party for everyone."

"I didn't think you were on fire. I just wanted to stop you in your tracks. Oh, Tommy, what have you done now? Mr Hampton, Mr Hampton, speak to me! Are you OK?" Ella rushed down the school steps, set the fire bucket on the pavement, and seized the limp wrist of the figure in the wheelbarrow. She dropped it just as quickly. "Ew! For goodness' sake, Tommy Crowe, that's not a dead body, that's a scarecrow." Her first aid training had clearly been better than mine.

Tommy raised his hands in indignation at the idiocy of grown-ups. "I never said it was a dead body, did I? Actually it's a guy, and I'm taking it to the vicarage ready for Saturday's party. What's your problem?"

Hector bent down and raised the frayed cloth cap covering the figure's face. "I know Joshua moves slowly, but not that slowly. It's a good likeness, though, I'll give you that, Tommy."

"That's not surprising. The clothes are all Mr Hampton's old ones. He gave them to me. I didn't take them." Tommy was clearly used to being

188

accused of misdemeanours, not always without good reason.

Hector turned on me. "Whatever made you think it was a dead body, Sophie?"

"Yeah, Sophie." Ella seized her fire bucket by the handle, jangling it pointedly.

I took a step back in self-defence. "How is this suddenly all my fault? I was only following a tip-off from Carol, who got the message from old Mrs Mason on the corner that Tommy Crowe had knocked Joshua Hampton down and carried him off in a wheelbarrow."

"Hello, hello?" a voice called from my telephone. I turned my back on the scene to reply.

"I'm so sorry, it's a completely false alarm. It's just a guy. You know, a Guy Fawkes guy. I do apologise for having troubled you." I pressed 'Call End' quickly before the operator could tell me off.

Hector let out a weary sigh. "Typical village Chinese whispers. That Mrs Mason's always been a bit hysterical. Carol ought to know better than to take her at her word."

"Especially since she's missing her nerve pills," said Ella. "I heard her giving poor Carol what for in the shop this morning because her prescription wasn't in her basket when she got it home. She's such a scatterbrain. Once she even left her false teeth on the counter."

"Well, how was I meant to know about Mrs Mason's nerve pills?" I asked crossly. "I was only following Carol's instructions."

Tommy turned on me, drawing on a childhood filled with classic teachers' admonitions. "And if Mrs

189

Mason told Carol to tell you to jump off a cliff, would you do it?"

To my relief, the others laughed at his impudence, and the tension began to dissipate.

Tommy looked how I felt. "Don't worry, miss," he said kindly. "People are always getting at me like that, too. You get used to it eventually."

Ella picked up the fire bucket and passed it to Tommy. "I tell you what, Tommy, if you sweep up the sand and put it back in the bucket, I'll let you off."

She flashed him her best smile, and Tommy visibly weakened. "OK, miss. I always did like you at school." I suspected Ella had a soft spot for him too.

I patted Tommy on the shoulder apologetically. "Sorry for all the fuss, Tommy. But well done on making that guy. It's a very good effort. He certainly had us fooled." I ignored Hector's arch look. "You and Joshua have done a great job."

Tommy feigned modesty. "Well, I suppose Mr Hampton did help a bit."

As Ella returned with the caretaker's broom, Hector glanced back up to our shop. "Come on, Sophie, back to work. You've left the shop completely unattended. The way this afternoon's going, we'll probably get back and find it full of masked men in stripey shirts with bulging swag bags."

As we strode back up the High Street together, Hector, irritated and uncomfortable, tried to brush the rest of the sand out of his hair. "Any other disasters while I was out?"

I shook my head, contrite. "No, just the one." I didn't like him being cross with me. I hoped I hadn't upset him enough to make him cancel our date. Even so, I was glad that things had worked out so well between Joshua and Tommy.

30 Shaking It Up

At least Tommy held no grudges against me for the fiasco with his guy. He turned up at Hector's House late the next afternoon jangling a pocketful of coins in his khaki parka. He marched in through the shop door and emptied them onto the main shop counter.

"Look what the vicar just gave me. Is it enough for a milkshake?"

Hector looked disparagingly at the pile of copper coins, began counting it, and gave up. It looked to me as if it amounted to less than fifty pence. A milkshake cost two pounds.

Hector pushed the coins back across the counter to Tommy and pointed to the Read for Good collecting box in front of the till. "I tell you what, if you put that lot into the charity box, I'll have Sophie make you a milkshake of your choice. And you can tell me why the vicar has been giving you his small change."

Tommy looked pleased with himself. "Banana, please, miss. I've been helping him all afternoon."

I calculated that must have been an hour at the most, by the time Tommy had got home from school and changed out of his school uniform. Even so, fifty pence seemed meagre wages for his labours.

"Helping him? By doing what?"

Tommy, enjoying posting coins in the orange box, spoke loudly so I could hear him over the clanking.

"Building his bonfire for Saturday."

I peeled and chopped a banana and put it in the milkshake blender with some milk. "What with? I thought he was having trouble getting enough wood for it."

"Turns out he didn't need much wood after all."

"Tommy, how exactly can you have a bonfire without much wood?"

"You don't need much at all if you've got plenty of books."

That made Hector tune back into the conversation. He nearly fell off his stool.

"What? No wood so he's burning books? That's the flimsiest excuse for censorship I've ever heard."

As I added a scoop of ice cream to the blender goblet, Hector followed Tommy over to the tearoom to extract more information. "Which books exactly? What kind of books? Library books? Ones from the vicarage shelves? Hymn books? Prayer books? Can you remember any of the titles?"

Tommy shrugged. "I dunno. All books look the same to me. It was fun, though. We made a big nest of them at the base of the bonfire, then put a little bit of wood on the top from the vicar's woodshed, with a big stake standing up in the middle to tie the best guy to. He's tied mine to it already, and he said I'd win the guy competition because I've been helping him."

He looked proud, and I was pleased for him, though it seemed unfair on those who hadn't yet delivered their guys for judging.

I decanted the contents of the blender into a glass, sprinkled the bubbly surface with grated chocolate, and added two straws before setting it in front of Tommy, who sucked at them eagerly. Hector made a T sign to me with his index fingers, and I took the hint to switch the kettle on

Only when the milkshake glass was half empty did Tommy come up for air. "Now we just need more guys. The vicar wants lots more guys to arrange all around mine."

Tommy paused to run a long, skinny finger around the inner rim of the glass.

"I had to show him the best way to make a bonfire, though. Honestly, you'd think he'd never made one before. He was so clumsy at it that I thought he was taking the mick, like he was pretending not to know how to do it so as to get me to do all the work. Lucky for him that I was there. Still, I didn't mind. I'm brilliant at making fires, my mum says. I always do ours at home. I think I could be a professional fire maker when I grow up."

Hector shot me a worried look. "I think you'll find the technical term for that is arsonist."

Tommy looked impressed. "Wow. I'll be one of them, then. My mum says I can get a Saturday job next year when I turn fourteen. Maybe I could work here?" He gazed around the shop as if taking it in for the first time. "It seems nice enough."

I brought two cups of tea to the table and sat down to join them, watching for Hector's reaction.

I could imagine Tommy quickly making himself at home here, camping out in a sleeping bag under the display tables because he liked it so much.

Hector's face was serious. "Not as an aspiring arsonist, you won't. Besides, the sort of person to whom all books look the same is probably not the best candidate for bookshop assistant."

"Fair enough." Tommy seemed undaunted. "Mum thought I might get a job mowing lawns. I always do ours at home. I've been thinking of setting up in lawnmowing. Running my own business, like you do, Hector." He tilted the glass to slurp up the rest of his drink.

"So have you got your own lawnmower, Tommy?" asked Hector. I was glad he was trying to point Tommy in the right direction, teaching him the basics of entrepreneurship.

Tommy set down his glass. "Well, my mum says I can't use ours as I'd wear it out and she couldn't afford to replace it. She says I should just use whatever the person's got whose lawn I'm mowing." He ran his finger around the inside of the glass again and licked it slowly. Although glad to see him enjoy his shake so much, I hoped he'd washed his hands after building the bonfire.

"Although I'm thinking of building a lawnmower myself. I mean, it can't be that hard, can it? All it has to do is cut grass. I could probably get hold of some old ones and make a whole new one out of them. That would be even better. I could be like James Dyson only with lawnmowers. Easy."

As Hector and I sipped our tea, I tried to picture the possible fruits of Tommy's engineering genius.

"Anyway, I can't stay here all afternoon chatting with you two." He lifted the lid of the sugar bowl to follow his milkshake with a sugar lump chaser. "I've got to finish the vicar's errand." He delved into his left parka pocket and extracted a thick stack of handwritten index cards. Pulling off the top one, he set it on the table between Hector and me. "There you go. Your official invitation for Saturday. The vicar was worried that not enough people have told him that they're coming to his party, so he's given me these to deliver." He pointed to the '+1' at the bottom left corner. "I'm not sure whether that means you have to bring one guy per person, or just another person. Do you want an invitation each or can you share?"

I let Hector respond. "One will do, thanks, Tommy. Sophie can be my plus one. But don't go getting mixed up and putting her on the bonfire."

Tommy didn't laugh, transfixed by the pile of cards in his hand. There must have been close to a hundred.

"I tell you what, I'll give you one each anyway. I've got to give them all out tonight, and it's going to take me ages."

He passed one across the table to me. The sight of the disjointed, childlike lettering, all in upper case, brought out the teacher in me. "He didn't get you to write all these as well, did he?" I wondered whether I ought to be offering Tommy some coaching to help him improve his handwriting.

"God, no. The vicar did them. It would have taken me months to do this much writing. I told him he ought to have done it on his computer and then

197

just print out loads to save all that writing, but he doesn't have one."

Hector looked surprised. "Really? I would have expected Mr Neep to have brought at least a laptop and printer with him. It must be a real chore to write all his sermons and correspondence by hand."

"My mum says that's how the rich stay rich. They're mean on the small things so they can save their money for the big things like Rolls Royces and swimming pools."

I found myself coming to Mr Neep's defence. "To be fair, Tommy, vicars don't earn much. He won't exactly have a champagne lifestyle." Joshua's getting through to me, I thought, with his call for charity.

"Which would be lost on a teetotaller anyway," said Hector.

"What's that mean – all he drinks is tea? Like you two?" Tommy nodded at our teacups.

"Not a bad guess, Tommy," said Hector. "It just means he doesn't drink alcohol."

Tommy scooped up the rest of the invitations and pushed back his chair. "Well, thanks for the milkshake." He felt optimistically in his coat pocket. "Sorry, miss, I didn't think to keep back any money to leave you a tip."

I suppressed a smile. "Thanks, Tommy, but don't worry. I'll count the invitation card as a very acceptable tip."

He brightened and headed for the door without looking back, intent upon his mission of delivering the rest of the vicar's invitations around the village.

Hector and I sat in companionable silence for a moment. The shop seemed to have grown bigger since Tommy left.

"He's a bit of a force of nature, isn't he?" I said eventually.

Hector gave a rueful smile. "Yes, but you need to keep an eye on him or he quickly gets out of hand. It takes the equivalent of sandbags in a flood to hold young Tommy back once he gets an idea into his head."

I read the card again. "Surely the vicar doesn't really mean everyone should bring a guy? The bonfire will look like an act of genocide."

"No, I think Tommy's got that wrong. I hope so, anyway." Hector sighed. "Poor old Tommy. I remember his dad vaguely. When I was a student, coming back to visit my parents here, he used to be in The Bluebird most nights. Seemed like a selfish git to me, though not without a certain charm. No-one was surprised when he walked out on Tommy's mum one day. Except Tommy's mum."

"Was there someone else involved?"

"No, he was just fed up with the responsibility of marriage and parenthood."

I looked closely at Hector to check for any signs of fellow feeling with Tommy's dad, and I was relieved to find there were none.

He drained his cup. "Better cash up now." He headed back to the bookshop till, while I checked the tearoom's cash drawer.

"So are you now thinking you might go to the vicar's party after all? Or were you just accepting Tommy's invitation to avoid hurting his feelings?"

Hector counted twenty pound coins into a plastic banking bag.

"I admit I'm tempted, if only to find out what books he's planning to burn." He opened the till with a ping and lifted out the cash drawer. "You're not trying to wriggle out of our meal on Saturday, are you, Sophie? I'm hoping the night will have a less traumatic ending than the PTA Halloween Disco."

I tried to sound playful and carefree so as not to reveal my nervousness about our impending night out. "Our third date. Third time lucky!" Only after I'd said it did I realise the implications.

Hector winked at me. "Sophie Sayers! Is that a proposition? Whatever would your old auntie say?" I knew he was only teasing me, but I couldn't help blushing. Hector chuckled as he counted up the rest of the day's takings.

31 Fun Guys

In the bookshop on the morning of Guy Fawkes' Night, Hector was busy laying out the last of the Guy Fawkes stock on the display table. After I'd sold a local map to a pair of American tourists who seemed keen to get out of the village as soon as possible, I remembered I'd never got round to looking up the book that the sales rep had been asking about earlier in the week.

"Hector, how do you spell Octavius, please?"

"In general, I don't. It's not a name I ever use." But he spelled it out anyway and I typed it in.

"France, I can handle," I said.

"What, all of it? Are you the new Joan of Arc? If so, you'd better leave the village before nightfall. She and bonfires did not get on."

Hector and I were both in something of a holiday mood, and I hoped his cheerful demeanour was for the same reason as mine: excitement about our imminent date.

"No, it's the surname of an author. Octavius France. There was a publisher's rep in here the other day asking whether we stocked his author's book, *Sentenced to Life*."

"That seems an odd question for a sales rep to ask a bookshop. His publisher's records would tell him whether we stocked it. He can't be much good as a rep."

"He did seem a bit clueless. He was wearing a very shiny suit. And lime green socks."

"Enough said."

I had to abandon my task as three families arrived at once, their children intent on spending birthday book tokens. I wondered what happened in the village each year to precipitate this cluster of autumn birthdays, and I had to bite back a smile when I heard one of the mums call her daughter Valentina.

After they'd gone, all tokens spent, the shop fell quiet for a bit. I allowed myself to fall into a little reverie as to what Hector and I might be doing next Valentine's Day, until he shouted across for my attention.

"Earth to Sophie. Tearoom, please!" It was a gentle reminder that he was still more boss than boyfriend, though I hoped our romantic meal that evening might ignite enough sparks to tip the balance the other way.

Hector had said we should go to the Chinese earlier rather than later, so we'd have time to go on to the Slate Green fireworks display after we'd eaten. He let me leave the shop a bit early to dash home to change into something other than the jeans and jumper that I'd worn for work. Fortunately, the rain had held off all day, and the first dry night in a week was forecast. I was glad not to have to worry that wet weather might put a damper on our date.

As I strode briskly home down the High Street, I was passed by a tandem heading the other way. I thought it odd that the second cyclist wasn't peddling at all until I realised it was a guy with a broomstick up its back to hold it erect. Then a young man passed by with a large guy over his shoulder in a fireman's lift. I regretted I wouldn't be seeing the full array of guys at the vicar's party later, but of course I wouldn't have swapped the lot of them for a night out with Hector.

Before I changed into a carefully chosen slinky Chinese silk dress of May's, insulated with thermal underwear (well, it was November), there was something important I had to do. I knocked on Joshua's front door to let him know why I wouldn't be going to the vicar's party. I didn't want him to think I was being rude or intolerant of the vicar.

I listened for his slow footsteps as he came to open his front door. In his front room behind him a log fire was already blazing in the grate.

"Ah, good evening, young Sophie. Looking forward to the fireworks tonight? Your eyes are alight already, I see."

I lowered my head, suddenly feeling shy, and looked up at him from under my eyelashes. "Actually, it's not the fireworks I'm looking forward to, but a meal out with Hector. We're going on a date."

Joshua gave me a knowing smile. "That comes as no surprise. I'm very happy for you both, my dear." Not much got past old Joshua. I asked him whether he would be going himself to witness the burning of the guy that he and Tommy had made together.

"I'm afraid I shall be spending the evening at home. Standing outdoors after dark in a crowd near a fire would be somewhat hazardous at my age. My eyesight is not what it was, and it would be all too easy for me to be the subject of an accident. I should hate to inconvenience the vicar by causing trouble."

I was touched by his thoughtfulness, yet saddened by the evidence of his ageing. "That's a shame. By the way, thank you so much for taking Tommy Crowe under your wing the other day. The guy you made was really effective."

"My pleasure, my dear, even if I did have to do nearly all the work myself. I confess I took a constitutional past the vicarage this morning to admire the sight of our guy atop the bonfire. It's in pride of place, you know, with others seated beneath it. It looks as though I am telling them all a story."

I smiled. "That sounds about right. I think quite a few more guys will have joined them since this morning, judging from the number being transported past Hector's House this afternoon. It was starting to look like a latter-day Black Death, with everyone bringing out their dead."

I decided not to tell him about the case of mistaken identity over his guy earlier in the week, and hoped no one else would either. Although he might have been flattered to know half the village had rushed to his aid before we realised our mistake, I didn't want to confront him with an image foreshadowing his own death, even if, as the oldest inhabitant of the village, he was likely to be the next to leave us.

I headed for the front door. He stood on the threshold of his cottage as I stepped carefully over the lavender hedge. Chivalrously, Joshua held his front door wide open to light my way and wished me a wonderful evening with Hector.

I paused with my key in my front door lock. "I'll be sure to tell you all about it tomorrow, over a nice cup of coffee." I looked forward to enjoying the evening all over again as I told him whatever proved fit for his old ears.

"I am sorry to have to stay at home, my dear, but I will at least be at the vicar's party in effigy, if not in spirit." He laughed gamely and I smiled. I had to admire his optimism. He gave me a final wave and called after me, "The vicar will have to wait a little longer to dispatch my spirit."

I fervently hoped that he was right.

32 Alone at Last

Five minutes after I'd changed, Hector pulled up outside my front door in his Land Rover. I pretended not to see Joshua watching us from his front room as I climbed up into the passenger seat. He had a fond but wistful look on his face. I supposed it was unlikely that he'd ever go out for another romantic dinner himself.

Hector suggested that rather than pore over the huge and complicated menu, we go for the set menu, which resulted in a constant trickle of sample size portions. I was glad the portions were small. My stomach was so tight with nerves that it felt like I'd just been fitted with a gastric band.

If we'd been stuck for something to say, guessing the ingredients and admiring the workmanship that had gone into the food would have fuelled our conversation. Even the garnish consisted of tiny works of art: roses chiselled out of radishes; chrysanthemums sculpted from carrots.

I picked up an exquisite rose and examined it. "If ever you want to bring me flowers, Hector, you could do worse than pick these."

He responded with a nervous smile.

Considering we spent all day, every day together in the shop without a moment's self-consciousness – well, not many moments, anyway – it was odd how transplanting ourselves away from home territory put us both on our guard. The restaurant's soft lights and gentle music were meant to put diners at their ease, but for us such an overtly romantic setting piled on pressure. Sharing dishes implied a certain intimacy between us that I wasn't sure Hector was ready for.

"OK, cards on the table time," said Hector abruptly, as the waiter took away the empty prawn cracker basket. "We might as well be honest with each other so we know what we're up against."

He made it sound like a battle. Seeing the disappointed look on my face, he immediately retracted.

"Well, not up against, but it would be helpful to know where we're each coming from with our previous relationships. I certainly owe you an explanation as to why I've been so backward in coming forward." He paused, unsheathing his chopsticks from their paper wrapper and snapping them apart ready for action.

The waiter set a dish of miniature starters between us. In silence, I waited for Hector to continue speaking. He said nothing, instead picking up a tiny pancake roll with his chopsticks and offering it up to me. As I took the whole thing in my mouth, I admired his superior dexterity with his chopsticks. I hoped I wouldn't have to resort to a knife and fork during the evening.

"Will it help if I go first?" I offered, once I'd finished chewing and swallowing. If he had a startling confession to make, he wasn't the only one of us who wanted to defer the moment.

He put his empty chopsticks to his mouth for a moment. "Yes, I think it would. Although of course you've told me quite a bit about your history with Damian already. Only tell me what you want to tell me. I'm still your boss, remember. If there are places you don't want to go, just say."

I brightened. "You know what that reminds me of? A Dr Seuss book that I was reading with Jemima this afternoon. 'Oh, the places you'll go—'"

I was pleased to be recommending a book to him for once.

"Does it have a happy ending?"

I nodded. "Yes, you should read it some time."

He picked up a little triangle of sesame prawn toast with his chopsticks and eyed it thoughtfully, as if trying to calculate the square on the hypotenuse.

"OK, then, I'll tell you about Damian and me. Just promise not to laugh. And in return I'll promise not to cry." He looked alarmed. "Joke," I said.

As we worked our way through a little basket of vegetables in tempura batter, I took him through my chequered history.

"OK, long story short. When I met him in Freshers' Week at uni, I was bowled over by his Viking good looks." Hector put his hand to his own dark curls, as if comparing himself with Damian.

"He had the confidence of a natural actor, but I was less than sure of myself. It was the easy option to stick with him all the way through to graduation, then to follow him out to Europe when he set up his touring drama company, Damian Drammaticas. It was his idea that I took a crash course in teaching English as a foreign language, so that I could earn money wherever we went."

Hector dipped a battered mushroom into a delicate pale bowl of dark spicy sauce. "It should have rung warning bells that he named his theatre group after an inflated version of himself."

I nodded, wondering why I'd never thought of that before.

"I was meant to follow them around Europe. It worked out the other way round. Instead of homing in on the hotspots for expats, where English-language plays might be welcomed, they gravitated towards wherever I was working as I moved from one international school to another."

I took a sip of green tea.

"Damian's version of the situation was that we were helping each other. He'd advertise my services to the audiences of his English-language plays, provided I sponsored the printed programmes. But I never got a single new pupil whom I could trace to one of his audiences. I tried to get more involved by writing skits and sketches for them, but Damian never took my writing seriously."

I laid my hands flat on the table to calm myself.

"I tried to make light of his derision, to tell myself it didn't matter, that he was right and that I wasn't really a writer. Even though Auntie May had always told me I had her writing genes, Damian completely undermined my self-confidence. While I was off travelling with him, I saw less and less of Auntie May, and so her belief in me lost its hold."

Hector reached across the table and covered my hands with his. I kept my eyes downcast, trying to hold back my tears. These things weren't easy to confess.

"It took Auntie May's death to make me realise how unhappy I had become. And your encouragement to get me writing properly again. May's legacy of her cottage was a welcome escape route. If she had lived to be a hundred, who knows when I'd have come to my senses about Damian?" I looked up. "Or met you?"

As I slipped my hands free of Hector's to dry my eyes on my serviette, he began to arrange slivers of cucumber and shreds of roast duck across a paper-thin pancake. Then he drizzled it with plum sauce and rolled it up with tight precision. I realised I was smiling through my tears.

"I think you've been spending too long in the bookshop's origami section."

"Yet another heathen religion, Neep would say." He leaned over the table to offer me a bite. I gladly accepted, savouring the cool, slithery cucumber against the spicy, hot meat.

Emboldened, I added an impromptu epilogue to my story. "And then I met a very nice man in a bookshop with whom I thought I might find a happier ending. Or at least share an interesting chapter or two."

Hector smiled faintly, busy toying with the frayed ends of a spring onion. It was cut so artfully that it wouldn't have looked out of place on a gift-wrapped parcel.

"Your turn now," I said gently, touching his hand. He looked up briefly, brow furrowed.

"OK, here goes. My story is similar, but different. I met Celeste in my final year at university."

Celeste? My heart sank. She sounded like an angel.

"Both reading English, we first noticed each other during a seminar in which we enjoyed a lively debate about Milton."

When he glanced up for reassurance, I tried to hide my dismay, but how could I compete with someone who could discuss Milton with him?

"That might not sound like a fast-track to romance, but it did it for us. We planned a gap year of travelling together after graduation, then we were going to return to do MAs, and maybe even doctorates, if we could both get places at the same university."

I was feeling stupider by the minute.

"While we were hitchhiking south through Spain, Celeste started to have abdominal pains. At first we assumed it was food-poisoning, or too much sun and sangria, but by the time we got to Gibraltar, on our way to Africa, she had lost so much weight that she could hardly stand. Everything seemed to go straight through her, of what little she could keep down in the first place."

He sat back to allow one waiter to light the plate-warmer in front of us, while another one deposited a cast-iron dish of sizzling beef in black bean sauce and an aluminium bowl of special fried rice.

"It turned out she had a rare stomach illness resulting in a growth the size of a grapefruit. By this time, she was so thin that I don't know how it fitted inside her."

I spooned some rice into my bowl, unsure about the beef.

"We cut our travels short, and on returning to England, she was rushed in for emergency surgery. At first it was touch and go as to whether she would survive. At the height of her illness, I proposed, saying I'd marry her whatever the prognosis. She played for time, saying she'd rather wait till she looked better in a wedding dress."

With a name like Celeste, I bet she'd look like a supermodel even in sackcloth.

"While she underwent prolonged treatment and several operations, I got a job in a local bookshop, but it didn't pay enough to support us both. Celeste was too ill to work, of course. So I thought I'd try my hand at writing books to earn extra income. Romance might not seem the obvious choice for a man, but I knew the genre sold in vast quantities."

This was certainly true in Hector's House.

"I never found a publisher or an agent willing to take me on, but I still kept at it. I suspect it was also wish-fulfilment. It's comforting to lose yourself in fictional happy endings when you're plummeting towards tragedy in real life."

He picked up the rice spoon and set it down again.

"You know George R R Martin's famous quote, '*The man who reads lives a thousand lives, he who doesn't read lives only once*'?"

213

I didn't, but I nodded anyway.

"Well, it works for writers too."

He took a deep breath. I sensed the worst was yet to come.

"By the time she was given the all-clear, we'd given up our plans for further study. Eventually she regained her lost weight, and her drive and her energy too. She took a job in our local public library, which was just right for her – not too strenuous, but quiet and rewarding – and we muddled along happily enough for a bit."

When he paused to tip some rice into his dish, I realised I'd been monopolising the beef and held the last piece up to his mouth with my chopsticks. He slipped it off with his teeth.

"Then one day out of the blue she announced that she was leaving me for someone else – one of the doctors she'd met in hospital. They'd been seeing each other ever since she'd been discharged, but she felt so obliged to me for my support during her illness that she didn't like to tell me."

Indignant on his behalf, I threw my chopsticks down on the table with a clatter. "Not so obliged that she wouldn't be unfaithful, though!" Secretly I was thankful, for without her infidelity my relationship with Hector wouldn't even have got this far. "So where is Celeste now?"

I watched him chase a fragment of noodle around his bowl with his chopsticks. Then he shrugged. "Australia somewhere."

The distance and vagueness of her location reassured me. She was even further away than Damian.

"Apparently it was easy for them to emigrate and start a new life there. They're always happy to have qualified doctors in places like Australia and New Zealand. I daresay she's got citizenship now. I don't know whether they have since got married. I'm not sure same-sex weddings are allowed down under."

"Same sex?"

"Oh, sorry, didn't I say? The doctor she ran off with was another woman. So you can see now why I'm cagey about relationships. She made me feel a failure as a man. I know I'm being stupid, but that's the way it is."

I covered my mouth with my hands. I hadn't seen that detail coming.

"After that, I couldn't bear to stay in our flat, and I quit my job in the bookshop too."

He fell silent for a moment, toying with his napkin, then forced a stiff, brave smile.

"But to look on the bright side, I'm thankful that I had those few years there, because it taught me enough to be able to set up my own independent bookshop. And the banter with the customers kept me going while Celeste was so ill. People were mostly very kind when they heard about my circumstances. Although like any bookshop, we had our fair share of nutcases. Can you believe a man once tried to get his money back on an Agatha Christie mystery because he'd worked out who the murderer was before he'd reached the end?"

I sensed that Hector needed to laugh after that gruelling confession, and so did I.

"And of course, the usual would-be authors demanding we stock the dreadful books they'd written, just because they lived nearby. Don't get me wrong, there were a few that were terrific. But the others just provided a work-out for my diplomacy muscles. Memoir writers are always worse than novelists, because they feel you're rejecting not only their books, but their lives. Strangely, we don't have many local authors wanting us to stock their books at Hector's House."

"Except one, but I hear his books are OK." I pointed to him and laughed. "Or rather hers, Miss Minty."

"Ah yes, well, present company excepted, of course. And maybe one day you, too?"

I pulled a face, not yet sharing his confidence in my ability as a writer. Despite having won two prizes, I was far from being a proper award-winning author.

"So an optimist would say I have a lot to thank Celeste for, because without her departure, I'd never have returned to the village to set up Hector's House. Her timing was spot-on, too, because my parents were just coming up to retirement. They wanted to give me their antiques business as a going concern, but I didn't have the requisite knowledge. I'd have sunk it in no time."

I nodded. I couldn't picture Hector running a dusty old antique shop.

"But I did know how to sell books, and I knew the village well enough, having grown up here, to curate the right mix of books to appeal to local customers, so they agreed to let me turn their antique shop into a bookshop."

I wondered what his parents were like, and whether I'd ever get to meet them.

"I moved back in to the flat over the shop with my parents while they looked for a retirement bungalow by the seaside. By the time my parents had their new home organised, we'd disposed of their stock and I'd refitted the shop with bookshelves. All that remains now from those days are the book display tables and the tearoom furniture, plus a few bits and pieces of vintage kitchenware and pictures."

I sat back in my chair, feeling full. "And what about your writing?"

"By this time, the technology had come in that allowed me to self-publish my romantic novels and sell them as ebooks." He laid down his chopsticks. "Once I'd mastered that, I started producing paperbacks too. I made sure, of course, that they were every bit as good as the others in the shop. Within about a year of moving back here, I started to make a reasonable profit."

I thought of all the other books in the shop besides Hermione Minty's.

"But how did you afford to buy in all the stock to start it up? That can't have been cheap." Once, during a quiet morning, I'd counted up roughly how many books were in the shop, and there were thousands.

Hector seemed impressed that I'd thought of that.

"I didn't like to ask my parents. They needed all their spare cash to buy their new bungalow. So I sought a sleeping partner to invest in initial stock."

I decided against making a joke about sleeping partners.

"May had always been a family friend, and she turned into my fairy godmother, loaning me enough to buy a start-up stock. My real godmother, Kate Blake, helped me with the refit. She's addicted to women's magazines and likes to think she's an interior design expert. To be fair to Kate, she did a good job. So there we are."

I hadn't realised that Hector and I would have so much in common. We'd both had the courage to start afresh, on the run from rubbish romances, taking refuge in a village that we regarded as a safe place.

33 Just Desserts

The waiter soon returned, this time bearing pale sorbet in frozen whole lemon skins. As we began to mine them with tiny spoons, Hector looked up imploringly.

"I'd appreciate it if you never mention Celeste to anyone, by the way. No-one else in the village knew what happened with her, apart from Kate and May and my parents. Everyone else thought I'd just come back to take over the shop so my parents could retire. No-one in the village ever met Celeste. She kept finding excuses to avoid meeting my parents, even at Christmas. I realise now that was because she had no intention of continuing our relationship long term."

I set down my spoon and sat back. "You know, I never brought Damian here, either. He wasn't interested in villages. He's more the city type, which I'm glad about now."

I was also glad Wendlebury could therefore be ours and ours alone.

Hector said he'd call for the bill. "Where's our waiter gone?" He surveyed the room.

"Was it that one over there?" I pointed to a short man dispensing lychees to a middle-aged couple in the far corner. I've never fancied lychees. They look like some bodily organ that's been surgically removed, though the waiter had tried to press them upon us as having aphrodisiac properties.

Hector shook his head. "No, he was taller with a little toothbrush moustache. I can't believe you didn't notice it. It's not a very common style these days." The kitchen door swung open, and we both turned to look. "Ah yes, that's him." Hector raised his hand, and the waiter nodded and went to prepare our bill.

"Gosh, you don't see many toothbrush moustaches like that these days, do you?" I mused, unable to take my eyes off it now that Hector had pointed it out. "Surely they went out of fashion with Brylcreem. I can't remember the last time I saw someone with one."

"Nor can I," said Hector, pulling his wallet out of his jacket pocket. "Wait – hang on. Yes, I can."

He slammed his hand down hard on the table, rattling the teaspoons in the sorbet dishes. Other diners looked across, probably wondering whether we were arguing over the bill.

"Picture this for a minute: the Reverend Neep, but with very short cropped black hair instead of the straggly white locks he has now, and beneath his long thin nose, the waiter's moustache. Do you know what that image conjures up for me?"

I tried to think of a famous person with short, dark hair and a toothbrush moustache. "Hitler?"

He shook his head. "No, but close. It reminds me of an author, leaning over the counter in the bookshop where I used to work, trying to press me to stock his dreadful memoir, and then practically spitting with rage when I refused."

"How funny!" I pulled a face.

"No, not funny at all," said Hector slowly. "Because this was no ordinary dull autobiography."

The waiter came and placed the bill in a little folder on a silver dish in between us. Hector picked it up, swept aside the mint chocolate sticks on top of it, glanced at the total and laid down five ten-pound notes.

"He'd been on trial accused of killing his wife in a bonfire in his back garden on Guy Fawkes' Night. There were no witnesses, and he claimed she'd fallen into the bonfire while he was indoors making a cup of tea. But whoever heard of someone having a bonfire party without inviting any guests? Although he proclaimed his innocence, forensic evidence strongly suggested that he'd done it, but some procedural cock-up by the local constabulary made it inadmissible, so he got off."

"Were there any children involved?" I asked.

"Fortunately not, but it was particularly galling for his late wife's brother, who was in the police force himself, but not allowed to be involved in the investigation due to their relationship. The poor man had a nervous breakdown after the trial was over and had to be sectioned. There are always more victims of a crime than meet the eye."

I arranged the chocolate sticks into a little pyramid that reminded me of a tiny edible bonfire. I thought they'd make a good cupcake topping, mentally noting the idea for the bookshop tearoom for subsequent Guy Fawkes' Nights.

"How awful," I said, letting Hector ramble on, thinking it would be a relief for us both to change the subject from Celeste.

"The author tried to sell his side of the story to the papers, but the whole business was so scurrilous that not even the tabloids would touch it. If he'd had any sense, he'd have thanked his lucky stars and slunk away to live quietly out of the public eye. Instead he wrote a book about it and got umpteen copies produced very badly by a vanity press. Once I'd refused to stock it, I never saw him in our shop again, and I presumed he'd left the area to start a new life."

I wasn't sure where Hector was going with all this and why he was telling me in such detail.

"There was a rumour that he'd gone mad with remorse for murdering his wife and killed himself, but I never believed that. He came across as too self-righteous, or at least too deluded."

"Hmmm," I said, now idly wondering whether Hector would notice if I ate more than my half of the chocolate.

"I never saw him again, until the day Mr Neep walked into Hector's House."

"What?" I choked for a moment, my eyes watering as I took a swig of cold green tea. "You mean that was Mr Neep?"

Hector nodded.

"Yes, that must be why he instantly took against me. He recognised me as one of the many booksellers who'd turned him down. I didn't make the connection until now, but why should I? An author doesn't meet many booksellers, but a bookseller meets hundreds of authors and publishers' reps over the years. He must be living in fear that I might remember him, despite his efforts to change his appearance."

I set down the tea cup and leaned back in my seat, drying my eyes with my napkin.

"Gosh. I'd never have thought a clergyman could be capable of murdering his own wife, or anyone else, for that matter."

Hector looked at me steadily. "The thing is, he wasn't a clergyman at all. He was a low-grade civil servant, working for the council. His only knowledge of the clergy was from his involvement with the amateur dramatic society, where he played the vicar in the Agatha Christie play, *The Murder at the Vicarage.*"

I sighed. "Oh God, not another actor. Honestly, I've had my fill of dramatic types. I don't care if I never see an actor again."

Hector raised his eyebrows. "That's going to make your nativity play a bit tricky, isn't it?" He pursed his lips. "Of course, I could be completely mistaken. I might have misremembered the whole thing, as it was a few years ago. I've got no evidence that our Mr Neep has done anything wrong apart from being annoying. It's only you that thinks he was the Grim Reaper, and even if he was, cutting a cable was hardly a criminal act. I'm being silly. I'm just letting my instincts run away with me."

"You should always follow your instincts, Hector," I said. I certainly did.

"I should hate to accuse a perfectly innocent man," said Hector. "It's highly likely that he's not

Septimus Vance at all. And supposing he is? In the eyes of the law, he's still innocent until proven guilty."

I set down my teacup with a thud. "Septimus Vance? Of course! That was the name of the author the publisher's rep mentioned when he came into the shop on Thursday. Not Octavius France at all. I bet it's him. And I bet the books he's burning on his bonfire are Septimus Vance's memoirs. He'll be destroying the evidence so he can start afresh with his new identify. No wonder Tommy said the books all looked the same."

Hector snorted. "A bonfire is all they're good for, if you ask me. But now I'm curious. I really want to get hold of a copy before they go up in smoke, or else we'll never know.

I spotted a snag. "But it's not illegal to change your name and become a vicar. A tragic bereavement like that could easily have made him turn to religion for comfort, whether or not he killed her. And you just said yourself that the best thing for him to have done after his release was to slink off quietly and start a new life somewhere else."

I couldn't believe I was actually defending Mr Neep. Joshua would have been proud of me.

"But given how much doubt surrounded his release, I still think we need to know. Well, I want to know, anyway. And even if he's not mad enough to set fire to anyone else in front of a crowd of people, if he is Vance, I think the diocese would want to know, too."

Hector glanced at his watch. "It's not yet seven o'clock, so he won't have lit the bonfire. Let's give

224

the Slate Green display a miss and get back to Wendlebury, pronto, before he destroys the evidence of his books on the bonfire. One book is all I want, Sophie. Just one book."

He scraped his chair back noisily, got to his feet and slipped quickly into his jacket. Heading towards the door, he called to me over his shoulder, "And you're right, sometimes I really should just follow my instincts. Now, let's go! I don't want to wait another moment!"

I pushed my chair back, stood up and hesitated.

"What about the rest of the chocolates?"

He glanced back, holding the door open. A chilly draught blew a pile of flimsy takeaway menus off the windowsill. "Bring them with you. You know what brand they are, don't you, sweetheart?"

I shook my head.

"Matchmakers."

I took it as a sign.

Grabbing my coat and handbag, I dashed out after Hector, telling the waiter, who had just materialised with a handful of coins on a silver salver, to keep the change. As I bolted for the door, I heard him declare to the cashier in astonishment, "And they didn't even have the lychees."

34 Some Guys Have All the Luck

Most of the villagers had come on foot so as not to drink and drive, so there was a free space on the road outside the vicarage, and Hector skilfully manoeuvred his Land Rover into it. Jumping down onto the pavement, I shivered as the chill night air penetrated my silk dress, glad that I'd slipped a small bottle of Auntie May's sloe gin into my coat pocket to share with Hector at the Slate Green fireworks display.

I'd never been to the vicarage before, but Hector knew his way round. As he led me past the prickly holly hedge and across the straggly front lawn to the side gate, rotting apples from the gnarled tree at the lawn's centre squelched under our feet, emitting sickly alcoholic fumes. The loud hum of chatter behind the high dry stone wall made it clear that plenty of people had got there before us.

"Looks as if all's well so far," I whispered to Hector as we turned the corner to find about a hundred people of all ages milling round the lawn and patio, dimly lit by flaming garden flares in the flower beds. Towards the far end of the lawn, at least fifty guys were arranged in a neat circle at the feet of Joshua and Tommy's guy. The latest arrivals were perched on the laps of the early ones. The bonfire seemed to be made almost entirely of paperback books, stacked half a dozen deep in the manner of a Cotswold dry stone wall. It had not yet been lit.

I heard Tommy's high voice among the crowd. "Can we light the bonfire yet, vicar?" Dissenters shouted him down.

"Not yet, please, Mr Neep."

"Shame to burn them so soon after all our hard work."

"Let's admire them for a bit longer."

"Do we even have to burn them at all?"

The vicar emerged briskly from the crowd, black frock swirling about his ankles. He rubbed his hands together, looking pleased with himself. "But the conflagration is the whole point of this celebratory occasion. Although if that is your communal wish, we shall refrain a little longer from its ignition until after the pyrotechnics."

Hector leaned in to me to speak in a low voice. "I remember thinking when I took a brief glimpse inside his book that he never used one syllable where five might do."

The vicar, meanwhile, seemed to enjoy being the centre of attention. "But first, let the games commence with competitive apple bobbing on the patio."

A swarm of children headed to the end of the patio where a row of plastic buckets filled to the brim with water were topped with mottled windfalls from beneath the tree in the front garden. I wouldn't have fancied clamping my teeth around any of those.

"Do you think they're poisoned?" I whispered to Hector. I thought no-one else had heard until Billy appeared, pressing up against me and speaking in an ominously low tone.

"*And the Lord God commanded the man, saying, 'Of every tree of the garden thou mayest freely eat, but of the tree of the knowledge of good and evil, thou shalt not eat of it: for in the day that thou eatest thereof thou shalt surely die'.*" He ended with a snake-like hiss that sent shivers down my spine. I let out an involuntary shriek.

Billy resumed his normal voice. "Genesis Chapter 2, verses 16 and 17," he said proudly, as if he'd just performed a party trick.

That should have made me feel less anxious, but it didn't.

Meanwhile Tommy Crowe had found his way to the front of the queue at one bucket. "Can I have a go? I'm brilliant at apple bobbing. I could be a professional apple bobber. And I have been helping you put men on the bonfire all day."

The vicar forced a laugh. "Guys, Thomas, guys, not men."

"Same difference," said Tommy, his eyes on the apples.

The vicar donned his black cloak over his frock for extra warmth. I nudged Hector and nodded at it, wondering whether I was the only one who recognised it as the Grim Reaper's. Even without the scythe or the hood, he looked sinister. I half expected him to announce that competitive neck-biting would follow the apple bobbing.

The vicar hauled a pocket watch from beneath his cloak as the first volunteers jostled by the buckets. "The fastest performer overall shall have as their prize a packet of sparklers. No contestant shall have more than ten seconds to attempt the feat."

A murmur of excitement swept across the patio, dominated by a cry of "Yes! Mine!" from Tommy. Like a boxing referee, the vicar roamed around as the children in turn struggled to pick out an apple with their teeth. Occasionally he patted their backs encouragingly, but when it came to Tommy's turn, he moved in close, his cloak falling like a vampire's might to conceal a victim from public view.

"Tommy!" I cried out in alarm. The vicar turned to stare at me accusingly before striding away into the shadows.

I realised Hector had disappeared from my side, and panicked until I saw him marching back towards me from inside the house, carrying two pale tumblers of murky liquid.

A noisy splash at another bucket heralded the surfacing of an elfin girl with red hair now sticking damply to her face, a worm-riddled apple in the mouth that smiled around it.

"Tommy's little sister," said Hector. There was applause from the crowd.

I accepted the tumbler he passed me and sniffed it suspiciously. "Anyway, where did you disappear to?"

He raised his glass to me and took a confident swig, which reassured me. "I've just been inside to check the lie of the land. The party's hardly started yet and already people are livening the punch up."

"There's been a punch-up? Oh no! Who's fighting?" I wondered whether the locals were taking the guy competition too seriously.

Hector shook his head slowly as if correcting a dimwit. "No, they're livening the punch. Up. Spiking it. Adding booze to the vicar's teetotal brew."

I clapped my hand over my mouth in horror. "What about the children? He can't feed alcohol to children."

Hector looked confident. "No chance of that. The vicar has bought in a few cases of the little fizzy pop bottles that Carol stocks. You know, the ones that look like samples from a 1960s paint card. The kids will always choose artificial rubbish with sports caps over liquid in a bowl with healthy bits of fruit in it. Nope, to the children their E-numbers, to the adults the booze. I just saw Trevor tip a whole bottle of brandy in it."

He raised his glass and took another enthusiastic mouthful.

"Your favourite tipple?" I made a mental note to get some in at home.

He nodded. "I developed a fondness for cognac when I was hitchhiking through France."

I suspected Celeste might have liked it too. Perhaps it had been their special drink.

I produce a little flask of May's sloe gin from my coat pocket. "What do you think of this, then?"

He peered at the label. "Ah, lovely. May's was always one of the best. I think she won a prize with it in the Village Show once or twice. I wouldn't mind being the judge of that competition class. As soon as the first frosts have been, we should take a stroll across the common and make our own for next year."

That he was assuming we'd be drinking it together next year warmed me up as much as a whole pint of sloe gin. I unscrewed the flask and savoured a sip before passing it to him. He didn't wipe the bottle clean before putting it to his own lips. It felt like a milestone in our relationship.

35 Hot Books

Another victory cry was raised up from the patio where a small boy had just retrieved an apple. With his dripping cheeks rosy from the cold night air and chilly water, he put me in mind of a suckling pig. Or a sacrificial lamb. The vicar was patting his head in a patronising manner.

"That little lad's currently favourite in the PTA's book," said Hector. "I heard them taking bets by the punch bowl. That big gap from his lost front teeth is deemed an unbeatable competitive advantage."

As I stowed my flask away, Hector put his arm around me and steered me gently towards the bonfire. "Come on, let's not get distracted from our mission. We must do what we came for. We must sneak one of the books the vicar's burning to prove whether he really is Septimus Vance."

We made our way through the still-growing crowds. When we reached the bonfire site, Hector crouched down to examine the paperbacks at its base.

"The spines are all facing inwards, as if he's trying to hide what they are. If that's not suspicious, then I'm Jeffrey Archer."

I bent down beside him and tried to pull a book free, then drew back when I felt a restraining hand clamp down on my shoulder.

"Don't do that, Sophie, you'll make the whole lot come tumbling down." I recognised the warm voice of our village policeman. Although my conscience was clear, the long arm of the law – well, Bob's long arm, anyway – made me nervous. I wondered how he ever got a date.

"What, like dominoes?" I stood up and turned round to face him, trying to form an innocent smile.

"Well, who's to say what it might do?" asked Bob. "I'm just on the lookout for issues of health and safety."

Billy sauntered up to join us, a brimming pint mug of punch in his hand. I recognised the glass from the pub. He must have brought it with him to ensure a large serving.

"*Health and Efficiency*? What, the nudist magazine? Are there copies of that on the bonfire?" He moved closer, ready to have a good look till Bob held him back.

"Now, now, I don't want any bonfires collapsing on members of the public, whether or not they're lit, on this most dangerous night of the year."

"I thought New Year's Eve was more dangerous, in terms of emergency service callouts," said Hector.

"Yes, but only because of all the alcohol that gets drunk."

Billy shook his head. "Ah no, you're wrong there, young Bobby. Depends where you spend it. I've managed to get quite badly injured spending a quiet night at home on New Year."

234

"Yes," said Bob, "because you fell down your cellar steps going to fetch your third bottle of sloe gin."

I gripped my little flask of the stuff tightly in my pocket, as if it might leap out of its own accord and incriminate me. I suspected Bob had a handle on every villager's vice.

"Still, there shouldn't be any trouble like that here," he said.

Suddenly worried whether the vicar might overhear us, I added loudly, "Because we all know the vicar's teetotal. I'm sure no harm will come to anyone at this party."

Bob leaned over to me conspiratorially. "I know, daft old bugger. That's why I'm planning to slip a bottle of my home-made crab apple wine into his punchbowl as soon as I get a chance. Sweet and smooth as a nut, it is."

Hector smirked. "Really, Bob? The rate the punch was disappearing when I was up there just now, I suggest you go and top it up before it's all gone." He drained his own glass and led Bob back inside, leaving me alone with Billy and his near-empty mug. I hoped Billy wouldn't stand too close to the bonfire. With that high an alcohol content, he'd be inflammable.

I turned and ran to catch up with Hector, overtaking Bob, who had paused to move one of the flaming torches at the side of the path to a less hazardous position.

"What about getting the books?" I hissed.

"Don't worry, Sophie, it's all under control. This is subterfuge. It'll distract Bob from the bonfire,

235

then we can go back and grab one while he's tucking into the punch and the snacks. Bob can never resist a free buffet. He'll fill his policeman's boots."

Hector led the way through the back door and the kitchen to the vicarage's large formal dining room, where a heavy oak table was laden with food and drink. At the centre was a large cut-glass punch bowl, immediately surrounded by a ring of old-fashioned snacks in cheap pressed glass dishes – crisps, twiglets, salted peanuts in various shades of beige. Expense had been spared.

Providing a pleasing contrast was a more colourful outer circle, like the petals of an exotic flower. Platters of all sizes were piled high with generous nibbles: slivers of pizza jewel-bright with peppers; hunks of cranberry-topped pork pie; traffic-light kebabs of red, yellow and green melon balls; cheeses dappled with every imaginable shade of fancy extra.

Bob chuckled at the sight. "It looks as if some of the guests didn't quite trust the vicar's standard of catering and sneaked in a few platters of their own." He headed off to fill a paper plate on an investigatory circuit of the table.

"I'm too full of Chinese food to eat a thing," I said to Hector through a mouthful of cantaloupe melon. "But I wouldn't mind another glass of punch."

"Go on, then," said Hector, holding out his own empty glass for a refill. "Then let's get back to the bonfire to nab our evidence before it goes up in smoke."

But as we returned to the lawn, the vicar was herding everyone away from the bonfire to stand back on the patio, directing them officiously. "Health and safety, health and safety!" That didn't sound like the cry of a murderer, unless it was a clever double bluff.

"Now, before we light the bonfire, it's time for sparklers to get you all in the mood for the big moment," he said. "All children under twelve, step forward." He reached into a capacious pocket of his cloak and pulled out a handful of short packets of sparklers. As a high-pitched cheer went up, I looked around for Tommy, expecting him to be disappointed at being excluded on grounds of age, but he was nowhere to be seen. I hoped he wasn't downing the punch. Tommy and alcohol would not be a good combination.

"But first the prize for apple bobbing goes to Laurence Jenkins. A whole packet of sparklers to himself."

The little boy with the big gap in his front teeth marched forward to a round of applause, receiving the paper packet from the vicar politely, before hissing loudly on his return to his mum, "You were right, they are only the short ones." His mother shushed him with a nervous laugh.

The vicar then called the rest of the children from the village school forward, dispensing a single sparkler to each.

"How do we light them, vicar?" asked one small voice.

Mrs Broom, the headmistress, stepped forward from the crowd. "Here, children, line up behind

Laurence and give me your sparklers one at a time. I'll light each one from this garden torch. Hands behind backs till I've lit yours. Then take it slowly to the middle of the lawn to play with it, keeping a good arm's length from the nearest child." She stretched her arm out in demonstration. "Once your sparkler's gone out, throw it carefully on to the bonfire and walk sensibly back to your parents."

As the children fell into line, I leaned across to Hector. "Do you think we can sneak back to the bonfire while they're playing with their sparklers? All the adults will be watching the kids for a bit."

Hector nodded. "Yes, let's pick our moment once they're all running about."

Soon it was as if there'd been an invasion of fireflies on the lawn as dozens of children darted about, pink-cheeked with the excitement of knowing the fiery thrill would be short lived. I watched them wistfully.

"I don't think you're ever too old for sparklers," I said, as we surreptitiously edged our way towards the bonfire. "I don't blame Tommy for being upset at being left out. I wish I had one."

Hector smiled. "Me too. I always think of sparklers as the warm-up exercise for the proper fireworks. They bring a pleasure out of all proportion to their size, because the experience is bound up with the anticipation of bigger thrills yet to come. They wouldn't be anywhere near so much fun afterwards."

I flinched as one or two children ran perilously close to the flares. "Maybe Mrs Broom should have made the children tie their hair back first, like we used to have to do for science and technology lessons to stop us inadvertently torching ourselves with Bunsen burners."

Too late we realised we'd missed our chance. Because the sparklers the vicar had provided were the shortest, cheapest ones, they all died out very quickly, and the children rushed forward to throw the bent bits of steel on the bonfire, making it the focus of everybody's attention. There was no chance of us raiding it unseen now.

36 Ignition, Blast Off!

The vicar emerged from the crowd again and raised his voice. "And now to ignite the conflagration, ladies and gentleman, boys and girls."

The crowd surged forward in anticipation, until the vicar held up his hands for silence. I thought for a moment he was going to say grace.

"Please, everyone, remain on the patio for your own safety, until the bonfire is well and truly ablaze."

"So we can all get thoroughly roasted after that," muttered a cynical voice at my elbow. "You'd think a vicar could choose his words more carefully."

"Hello, Dinah. Having fun?" I asked.

"Hmm, well, I'm enjoying the punch bowl." The Chair of the Wendlebury Writers raised her glass to me. Her girlfriend – the same lady that I'd seen with her at the Village Show drinking chardonnay from a bottle through a straw – nodded her agreement. I saw from her glass that the colour of the punch had changed since we'd got ours. I raised mine, nearly empty now, in return. I liked this lady, who seemed to be brightening Dinah's outlook on life a little.

"Stand well back, children." Mrs Broom's voice became uncharacteristically high pitched as the vicar uprooted a flare and held it to the row of books at the base of the bonfire.

The crowd held its collective breath, waiting for the first flame to catch. "I'm going to have to sneak round to pull one out from the back," Hector whispered, sidling away from me. "If you need to, create a diversion so no-one sees me. Perhaps pretend to faint."

The flare continued to blaze merrily, but summoned only a little puff of opaque dove-grey smoke from the uncooperative books.

"Must be *Fifty Shades of Grey*," said one of the dads in the crowd, and all the adults laughed, plus more of the teenagers than ought to have got the joke.

"They're probably too densely packed to go up in flames." I recognised Trevor's voice of authority as a responsible builder used to disposing safely of waste. "Not enough oxygen in between the layers. Still, they'll protect your lawn when the fire does eventually take off, vicar. Keep it cool beneath the ashes. It'll be nice and green in the morning when you clear them all away again."

"You'd do better to start by igniting the guys rather than the books." This was Stanley. "Their straw stuffing should go up a treat, and the rest of the bonfire will soon catch."

The vicar, apparently enjoying the attention of an unusually large congregation, began to work the crowd as if he was playing pantomime, which was surprising, considering he'd just banned the school's one. Stagily, he feigned coyness.

"All these beautiful guys? No, I don't think so. Not after all the time you've spent making them, my friends." He lowered the flare theatrically. "Do you think so?"

He raised it teasingly towards Joshua's guy's flat cap. "Maybe I'll just give him a bit of a headache, eh?"

A couple of mums at the front of the crowd covered their young children's eyes with their hands.

"Oh dear me, I can't decide! What shall I do?" The vicar left an empty silence, which of course the crowd was happy to fill. "Burn him! Burn him!"

I heard Dinah muttering beside me, "Bloody savages."

Her girlfriend put one hand on her arm in comfort. "Not really, Dinah. You know they're all perfectly nice."

Dinah raised her eyebrows dismissively. "It smacks of *Lord of the Flies*, if you ask me."

We all gazed at the fire, transfixed. The vicar continued to wave the torch around the Joshua guy like some kind of medieval torturer, totally in control of his audience.

Suddenly he lost the upper hand. Not literally – I don't mean he set fire to himself. But from within the bonfire came a terrible roar, and a familiar figure in a khaki parka rose from the mound of scarecrows at the vicar's feet.

Tommy Crowe had patiently concealed himself among the guys while the rest of us were watching the children play with the sparklers. He raised his arms and roared like a cartoon King Kong, eliciting screams from the crowd. Several small children and one or two mums burst into horrified tears. The vicar dropped the flare on his foot and immediately had to stamp hard on it with the other one to extinguish his flaming shoelaces. Then he recovered himself, retrieved his still burning flare and held it up over his head threateningly, as if about to lead Transylvanian villagers to storm Baron Frankenstein's Castle.

"Tommy Crowe! Is that your gratitude for all the kindness I've shown you this last week?"

Tommy stepped down from the pyre, dusted himself off and shot the vicar a withering glance. "Can't you take a joke?"

He strolled off nonchalantly into the crowd, where he was variously slapped about the head by defensive mums of small children and patted on the back by teenagers and those adults who enjoyed a good fright now and again. Others were laughing and heckling.

"Trust Tommy Crowe to keep the vicar on his toes."

"Serve him right."

Dinah's girlfriend took a more conciliatory approach. "It would have saved a lot of trouble if the vicar had just given the boy a sparkler."

I hoped she was going to stick around.

Eventually the hubbub died down, and the vicar regained his composure. He held the flare aloft once more to command the crowd's attention.

"Now, seeing as I'm not having much luck, perhaps someone else would like to do the honours? I don't see why I should have all the fun. Tommy?"

Impressed by the speed of what I hoped was the vicar's forgiveness, I was disappointed when it became clear that Tommy was no longer in earshot.

I assumed he had slunk off home, contrite, or been sent home in disgrace by his mother.

"Anyone care to volunteer?" asked the vicar, and dozens of small hands shot up.

Mrs Broom gestured to the children to lower them again. "I think we'd better leave this to a grown-up."

Then Billy was pushed out into the clearing by several of his drinking pals. "Go on, Bill. You always liked playing with matches!" In that moment, I realised Billy must have been the Tommy Crowe of his generation.

Billy put up a brief and unconvincing display of resistance before trudging forward, his wellies leaving pudgy footprints on the damp grass. Accepting the vicar's proffered flare, Billy made a big show of walking around the front of the bonfire a couple of times, searching for the most likely place to start. Neep meanwhile disappeared into the shadows.

When Billy touched the flare to some of the guys, he succeeded only in shedding light on them rather than setting them on fire. "Too bloody damp, vicar. We're going to need a bit of help." He turned to appeal to the crowd. "Anyone got any petrol on them?"

There was a surge of admonitions at his characteristic recklessness, probably one reason for his reputation since boyhood.

Billy waved away the crowd's derision. "Only joking, ain't I?" He stepped forward again, torch held out in front of him. He was well camouflaged by the pile of battered figures in frayed clothes.

"Hang on, though, there's one here that looks a bit too lifelike for my liking."

More catcalls from the crowd.

"Not as funny second time round."

"Been there, done that."

"Run out of jokes of your own?"

Just then, Hector emerged from behind the bonfire. He detoured to me, pulled one of my hands behind my back, and pressed what I could feel was a book into it.

"Keep it hidden," he hissed.

Meanwhile Billy had pulled himself up to his full height and plunged the flare back into the ground beside him. "Well, I'm having its shiny shoes first. No point burning 'em."

Stanley peeled off from the crowd, directing his torch on to the guy's feet like a spotlight to give Billy a second opinion on the shoes.

"You're right, Bill, they're too good to burn."

Billy jostled up against him. "I saw 'em first, Stan. If they're my size, I'm taking 'em off his hands."

"Feet," said Stanley. "You mean feet."

Billy bent down, removed the guy's shoes and held them up to show the crowd like a trophy. If this was going to turn into a low-budget makeover for Billy, it might take some time.

Stanley swung the torch back on to the unshod guy.

"Not sure about his socks, though," he added. "A bit garish for you, Bill."

I let out a scream.

246

Hector grabbed my arm and hissed in my ear, "It's OK, Sophie, no need for diversion tactics now. We've got the book, and we were right about it."

Trembling, I backed away, pointing at the guy's familiar lime green feet. "I recognise those socks. That's no guy. It's the publisher's rep who was in the bookshop on Thursday. He told me he was on his way to the vicarage, but it looks as if Mr Neep's murdered him."

Without a moment's hesitation, Bob stepped forward from the crowd, pushed Stanley and Billy aside and bent down to reach up inside the unshod guy's trouser leg. I wondered for a moment whether it was a party trick, and he was about to produce the guy's underpants without removing his trousers. Then he leapt to his feet in surprise, and turned to slap Billy on the lapel with the back of his hand.

"Sophie's bloody right, mate. This one is as much flesh and blood as I am."

37 The Warm-up Guy

"No wonder those shoes were a bit whiffy," said Stanley.

Bob bent down once more and laid a hand on the bare ankle.

"Whoever he is, he's a damn sight colder than he ought to be, but I don't think he's quite dead yet." He tugged on the rep's legs to wrench the body from beneath the pile of guys and dragged him on to the lawn, where Billy ripped off the plastic mask that had been used to disguise the man's face. I crept a little closer to scrutinise his features.

"That's the rep all right," I faltered.

"And this is Septimus Vance," said Hector, taking the book back from my hands and holding it aloft to display the title to the crowd. "The alter ego of the Reverend Neep, who a few years ago was tried and found innocent of murdering his wife in a bonfire, after the case was thrown out of court due to some procedural errors." He turned the book round to show the author photo on the back, undeniably Mr Neep. "Though why he'd want to murder a publisher's rep I have no idea."

I stepped forward. "I can prove the rep's identity too. He's bound to have business cards in his pocket. Reps always do." I knelt at the unconscious man's side, slipped my hand into his jacket pocket, and with a flourish pulled out a black plastic card case. I flipped it open and held it up victoriously. "See?"

Hector steadied my hand to examine the card case by the light of his torch app. "Actually, I think you've just proved that he's not a rep at all, but a policeman. That's a police detective's ID card for one Detective Constable Simon Yardley." He looked up. "I remember now from the newspaper reports, that was the name of Vance's brother-in-law. I'm guessing he came here in plain clothes, hot on the trail of Septimus Vance under his new identity, though not quite as hot as Vance had planned him to be."

Bob took the card from him to examine it. "Nope, that style of ID card was superseded a few years ago. He won't have been here on official police business. In any case, a detective would be unlikely to operate alone, and he certainly couldn't disappear for a couple of days while on a case without someone noticing."

"Perhaps he left the force after his breakdown following Vance's trial," said Hector. "He was convinced Vance was guilty and must have come to seek private retribution."

"Goodness, how horrified he must have been to discover Vance had disguised himself as the Reverend Neep," I said.

"I bloody told you Neep weren't a proper vicar," said Billy indignantly. "I knows a proper vicar when I sees one!"

"But why try to pass himself off as one?" I asked.

Hector looked stumped. "I really don't know. But let's worry about that later. First priority is to check that Yardley of the Yard here hasn't been another murder victim."

Stanley marshalled the crowd to tend to the casualty. "OK, folks, clear a space. Let's get him up to the patio for a bit of first aid while he's still breathing. Larry, Ron, Trevor, Steve, go and dismantle the rest of the bonfire, would you? We'd better make sure there aren't any more dead bodies tucked away in there."

Bob slipped Simon Yardley's card into his own pocket. "And I think I'd better take Mr Neep into custody for questioning in connection with the attempted murder of Mr Yardley here."

But Septimus Vance was nowhere to be seen.

38 Not Much Cop

Soon all the other guys lay in neat rows across the lawn, making it look like a makeshift battlefield morgue. It took a while for a team of volunteers to confirm that none of them had ever had a pulse.

The crowd parted like the Red Sea to allow Stanley and his team to carry DC Yardley to the patio, where they lay him down on a picnic table bathed in security lights. Many of the villagers, fearing the worst, retreated indoors, parents with their arms around sobbing children.

"These naughty men have spoiled our bonfire!" wailed one small boy. I was glad that the true reason for the destruction of the bonfire had passed him by.

Holding tightly on to Hector's hand, I crept forward towards the inert figure. As we got close enough to see, I clapped my hand over my mouth too late to mute a loud gasp of horror. He looked in a very bad way, a shadow of the man I'd met in the shop.

Billy looked at me over his shoulder.

"Go on, girlie, let it rip. That might bring him back from the dead. Got any smelling salts on you?"

"When was the last time women carried smelling salts in their handbags?" asked Dinah, who had followed close behind me. "Smelling salts, my foot!"

Billy was unperturbed. "Well, if you've got smelly feet, take your shoes off and walk this way. That might do the job just as well."

Dinah's girlfriend sweetly came to her defence. "She really hasn't, you know."

Bob returned after a circuit of the garden, unable to find Vance, and radioed for police reinforcements before going off again to continue his search. Meanwhile, Carol phoned the village doctor, who was spending the evening at home. He didn't care for fireworks, having seen too many times the injuries they'd caused. On arrival at the vicarage, the doctor quickly checked the detective's vital signs, found a faint pulse in his neck, and called an ambulance. Then he called me over for more information.

"So, what do you know about our friend here, Sophie?"

"Nothing at all. Even what I thought I knew was wrong. I assumed he was a publisher's rep when he called into the shop asking about a local author I'd never heard of. No wonder he didn't seem much cop at his job. When he left the shop, he told me he was meeting a friend at the vicarage."

Hector came to join us, waving the book he'd retrieved from the bonfire. "This won't tell you about Detective Constable Yardley, doctor, but it will tell you more about who he was looking for."

He held up the back cover to show a photo of an airbrushed younger Mr Neep with jet black hair and a toothbrush moustache. "This is Septimus Vance, who tried to palm me off with a box full of his abysmal autobiographies a few years ago, in the bookshop I worked in before Hector's House. He is an arrogant and unpleasant man, and it looks like he tried to disguise Simon Yardley as a guy and dispose of his body in the bonfire."

Carol was fanning her face with a paper plate. She must have realised she'd had a lucky escape.

Hector gazed at the photo on the book again. "Vance looked very different back then, but even so, I'm kicking myself for not recognising him. Perhaps I could have prevented all this unpleasantness. I'm sorry."

Billy quickly came to Hector's defence. "It's not your fault, young Hector. I blame the bloody Bishop. Why would the diocese send us a suspected murderer to tend to its flock? And if you're going to pretend to be someone else, why pick a daft name like Neep? I mean, if I were going to change my name, I'd make it something rugged like De Niro. Or I could be Billy Depp."

The doctor, meanwhile, continued to monitor DC Yardley's vital signs. He held open his patient's eyelids in turn, peering into them with a small medical torch.

"I think he's been heavily dosed with some kind of sedative or relaxant for a day or two, which accounts for why Neep's been able to keep him here since Sophie saw him in Hector's House. I'm guessing Neep slipped him a spiked drink not long after you met him, Sophie, before hiding his body under the bonfire."

It seemed a convoluted way to go about killing someone.

"But if he wanted the man dead, why didn't he just give him a bigger dose?" I asked the doctor.

"It seems his intention was to place the blame on someone else – on whoever he could get to light the bonfire. Thank goodness you spotted him, Sophie, or Neep might have got away with it. Thanks to you, DC Yardley is not dead, but he is hypothermic. That's not surprising considering he's been lying outside in a thin damp suit for a day or two, but I don't think any lasting damage has been done."

"So that's where Mrs Mason's nerve pills disappeared to," Carol said crossly. "I knew I'd given them to her. I thought she'd just lost them at home, but now I think of it, the vicar was in the shop at the same time as her. He must have swiped them out of her shopping basket while she wasn't looking. And him a man of the cloth too!"

"But that was on Monday, days before Mr Yardley showed up," I said. "Crikey, I wonder who else he had murderous designs on."

The doctor tutted. "Dear me, I wish people would take better care of their prescription medicines. This poor young man will feel he's got the mother of all hangovers when he wakes up, but our first priority is to warm him up slowly, while we get him to hospital for proper checks and observation." He pinched the flesh on the back of the detective's hand, and it stood up in wrinkles, despite his young age. "They'll need to get a drip into him for rehydration too."

Someone handed Carol an eiderdown from one of the vicarage guest rooms, and she tucked it carefully around the detective's body. The tender gesture reminded me of the many years she had spent caring for her stricken mother. She had such a good heart, I was so sorry her hopes for romance with the vicar had been dashed. But Carol was never daunted for long.

"He looks a nice man," she said thoughtfully, stroking the detective's hair.

"Anyone check his pockets for personal possessions other than his police ID?" asked the doctor. Carol didn't need to be asked twice. She delved beneath the eiderdown for a little longer than strictly necessary before withdrawing from his trouser pocket a wallet and a mobile phone.

The doctor took the phone. "Dinah, can you please put that on charge? Once it's powered back up we'll find his home contact number. Someone somewhere is probably very worried about him not having been home for a couple of days. I see he's wearing a wedding ring."

Carol's face fell, then she remembered Neep. "But hang on, where is Mr Neep now? I hope he's all right."

Billy shook his fist at her. "Don't you go sparing no sympathy on that scoundrel. He damn near set me up to be a murderer. Supposing that fire had caught light? It would have been me who done the awful deed, in front of the whole village, setting fire to that young man you're cuddling there. And who would take my word over the vicar's?"

"I would."

"And me."

"Me too."

The crowd's unanimous agreement seemed to touch Billy. "Well, I thank you for that, you're all very kind. Now, where's that vicar got to? Let's lynch the bugger."

He seized a garden rake from the nearest flowerbed and stumbled off down the lawn towards the vegetable garden beyond, reminding me of Mr MacGregor chasing Peter Rabbit.

Stanley hurried after him. "Now, now, Billy, don't do anything rash."

"Who's got a rash?" Tommy entered the garden at the side gate, his jaunty tread indicating he was undaunted by his latest exploits. He saw Stanley leading Billy back to the patio by the sleeve as if restraining a naughty schoolboy.

"What you done now, Billy?" Tommy recognised a kindred spirit when he saw one.

Billy shook himself free of Stanley as Bob returned from the far end of the garden.

"Where's that bloody vicar?" asked Billy. "I wants a piece of him."

"So do I, Bill, but I can't find him anywhere," said Bob. "That black cloak of his is certainly a good disguise on a dark night like this. I hope my reinforcements will be here soon, before he can get too far."

Tommy was quick to reassure Bob. "Don't worry, he won't have got very far at all. I let his car tyres down again while the little kids were playing with their sparklers."

"Well done, sonny."

258

I hoped Tommy wouldn't take Bob's approval as licence to vandalise any other vehicles in the village.

"Last time I saw him, he was running up the path into the church, then he went inside and slammed the door behind him. He'd gone round the back way, cutting through the gate at the bottom of the vegetable patch, so he didn't notice me at the other end of the path, where I was trying to set fire to the lychgate."

"What?" Relieved as he was, Bob couldn't let that one go. "Whatever possessed you to do that, Tommy? Don't tell me I've got to call the fire brigade too?"

Tommy dismissed the offer with a casual wave of his hand. "I just thought it might be useful for the vicar to know how easy it was to set light to it. So as to guard against accidents. You know, for that health and safety you're all so keen on. But don't worry, it's practically impossible. I got bored trying and came back here to get something to eat. I'm starving." He stared longingly in the direction of the dining room.

Bob put his hands on his hips. "Ha! I've got bigger fish to fry tonight than you, my lad. Off you go."

"That's all right, Bob, I don't like fish anyway. Yuck."

Tommy ran off happily to join the villagers now tucking into the buffet inside the vicarage, leaving Bob looking anxiously towards the church.

"We'll go with you if you like," said Stanley, speaking on behalf of the small crowd of his cronies that had gathered round him with drinks and plates of snacks. "You don't want to go on your own."

"No, I shouldn't encourage civilians to get involved, in case he is armed."

Billy looked scornful. "What, you think he might come at us with a Roman candle?"

Bob considered. "You can't come inside, but you can stand guard outside the church door till reinforcements arrive, if you like. And I don't suppose there's any harm if anyone wants to watch the proceedings from the churchyard. Just don't make any loud noises to alert Neep to our presence."

The men could not contain their roar of enthusiasm as they set off down the path after Bob, still carrying their drinks. Bob shouted back over his shoulder to us.

"And don't start the fireworks till we've nabbed him."

"I thought they were meant to be keeping the noise down?" I said to Hector in a low voice. "I can't believe we're still going ahead with the fireworks."

Dinah's girlfriend shrugged. "It seems a shame to waste them, when they're all set up ready to light behind the bonfire."

Carol looked up from her patient's side. "And it seems a shame to waste a good opportunity for a party. Especially when we've all brought so much food and drink."

"There's tons to eat in there," said Tommy, returning with a cold chicken leg in each hand. "And it's funny, but my mum says she keeps drinking the punch but it never seems to get any less. She'd like a bottle of wine like that for home. Has the vicar done something magic to it? I hope he's done the same thing to the food."

"You're thinking of miracles, Tommy, and no, vicars can't do miracles," said Carol. "We really need to get Sunday School up and running again once we get our new vicar."

Hector coughed. "I saw Trevor top the punch up earlier with a drop of brandy, and Bob stuck in a bottle of his crab apple wine."

"Then there's my bottle of Malibu," said Carol. "And some foreign green liqueur that May Sayers brought my dad years ago." She turned to address me. "I'm sorry, Sophie, but it had been there a long time, and I was never going to drink it, so I thought I might as well share it with the village."

I produced the little flask from my coat pocket. "But don't worry if the punch starts to run low. I've got some sloe gin."

Everyone laughed, and somebody hiccupped. I don't think it was me.

"So I think you have your answer, Tommy," said Hector. "The magic lies not in the hands of the so-called vicar, but in the rest of the village community. When we all pull together, there's nothing we can't do." Just then, through the gaps in the holly hedge, blue flashing lights appeared beside Hector's Land Rover. "But if any of you came here by car tonight, for goodness' sake, make sure you walk home or you'll be done for drunken driving."

Then he grabbed my hand. "Come on, Sophie, let's go and see the vicar get his comeuppance, though I suppose we should stop calling him that now."

We crept quietly out of the garden and headed next door to the lychgate, arriving just as Bob's reinforcements were running up the path to the church. As they opened the porch door, we heard a cry of "Sanctuary!" from within.

Hector spoke derisively. "That might have worked for Quasimodo, but Vance is about five hundred years too late."

The door slammed behind the police, leaving an ominous silence. "Do you think he's armed?" I whispered to Hector, bracing myself for the sound of gunshots, or at least the sound of bangers. Hector rubbed my back soothingly.

"I don't think that's his style somehow. I'm sure they'll all come out in one piece. Don't worry, sweetheart."

Whatever happened next, I knew I'd cope better with it as Hector's sweetheart.

39 Flash Mob

We'd been crouching by the lychgate for about five minutes when Bob led out Mr Neep – or rather Septimus Vance – in handcuffs. Bent over, humiliated, he looked at least ten years older than when he'd fled from his garden. I wondered what the police were charging him with: threatening behaviour at the PTA Halloween Disco; damage to the disco equipment; the theft of Mrs Mason's prescription drugs; sedating and holding captive a detective; attempting to induce a member of the public to murder the sedated detective. The prosecution would be spoiled for choice.

But what I found the most unnerving was that he had somehow got the whole village to do his bidding. What else might he have had planned for us? Even so, I'd never felt safer than here, now, in the company of an unrepentant criminal. In a big city, he might have stood more of a chance of success, but not in Wendlebury Barrow.

Vance stopped walking as he reached the lychgate, forcing Bob to grind to a halt too. Emitting a surly growl, he slowly surveyed our faces as if memorising them for future reference and revenge. Hector tightened his arm reassuringly around me, but Billy was less easily cowed than I was. Standing up to his full height, he fished out of his trouser pocket a battered packet of cigarettes, put one in his mouth, and tauntingly raised a lit match to it.

Vance watched him, transfixed by the flame like a caveman desperate for the gift of fire. Billy took a long draught, puffed the smoke out of his mouth with a satisfied smirk, and stepped closer to the vicar.

"Now I'm going back to enjoy a bloody good piss-up at your house," he said with relish. "And I might even sleep in your bed."

Vance gave a shudder of rage, and Bob yanked on his handcuffs to start him walking again, accompanied by the rest of his boys in blue. "We'll be back to take your statements in the morning," Bob called over his shoulder. "Don't wait up. Just enjoy a good party. Because the party's all yours now, my friends!"

Once the police cars had driven off to Slate Green Police Station, we headed back to the vicarage. Hector and I entered the garden by the back gate just in time to see Billy chuck his glowing cigarette end behind the bonfire, where it landed on what turned out to be Neep's stash of fireworks. At the first explosion, people rushed out of the house, food and drink still in hand, and before long we were all gathered on the patio, oohing and aahing at the pyrotechnics. I mean fireworks. Blast that vicar and his pompous way with words.

"What about the bonfire?" asked Tommy when the last sparks had died down. "Should we stick all the guys back on it and set light to it now?" He pulled a box of matches out of his pocket. The rest of us exchanged nervous glances.

Then Trevor had a bright idea. "I know. Let's just use them as scarecrows instead. It seems a shame to burn them after everyone's gone to so much trouble."

Tommy turned appealing eyes on me, and he sounded shy for once. "Do you think I'd be allowed to put Mr Hampton's guy in my garden, or do you think he'll want it back?" I thought of Joshua and his father, effectively a human scarecrow at Tommy's age. Then I looked at Tommy, missing a father figure for most of his short life.

"I'm sure Mr Hampton will be delighted to know he's going to such a good home. Much better than turning him into a pile of ash."

Tommy looked the happiest I'd ever seen him. "Thanks, miss, I knew you were a good sort. Have you ever considered becoming a teacher?"

I tried not to smile. "Funnily enough, Tommy, the idea had crossed my mind."

At the sound of pop music blaring out of the kitchen, where the teenagers had started dancing, Tommy ran off inside in search of whatever mischief might be to hand.

Meanwhile, Detective Constable Yardley had regained consciousness and had been raised into a sitting position on a garden bench on the patio, the eiderdown spread over his lap. Carol, still holding his hands, was chatting companionably to him in a low voice. More blue lights flashed in the High Street, signalling the arrival of the ambulance.

Carol watched as the paramedics carried the detective off to the ambulance on a gurney, then, with a heartfelt sigh, she went inside to join the others.

Hector and I were following her across the patio when we were accosted by a middle-aged lady I'd never met before. She seemed to know Hector, though, as she reached up to kiss him on both cheeks with the manner of a fond aunt. He let go of my hand to give her a hug.

"Hello, Kate. Welcome home. Are you still on Australian time?"

I realised she must be his godmother, back from her long holiday.

She let out a sigh. "I think so. We got back in the early hours of this morning while the rest of the village was asleep, and I've been catnapping all day. I don't know which way is up yet, which seems appropriate enough considering where I've just come from. Then the banging and crashing up here woke me, so I thought I'd better get out of holiday mode, put my Parochial Church Council hat on, and come and investigate. I feared squatters had invaded the vicarage while it was empty."

"No, only the new vicar."

"Mr Neep? It can't be. He's still in hospital in Southampton."

"Well, that was quick. They've only just taken him away in a police car."

"No, really, Mr Neep is in hospital in intensive care and has been for weeks. He was beaten up and left for dead by an intruder. The attacker stole his wallet, his passport, and all the other personal

266

paperwork that he could find, in what looks like a planned identity theft."

"But we've had the new vicar, Mr Neep, here for the last three weeks. Only it turns out his real name is Septimus Vance."

Kate's eyes widened. "Septimus Vance? But that was the name of the man suspected of being Mr Neep's assailant. I had an email from the diocese a couple of days before I left Australia to let me know about poor Mr Neep's situation, and that his arrival would be delayed while he recovered. They asked me to keep it a secret while they investigated. They even managed to keep the story of Neep's attack out of the papers, to try to fool his attacker into thinking he'd escape undetected."

"But why didn't they tell you sooner?" I asked. "Septimus Vance has been here for weeks."

"No-one realised anything was amiss until a few days ago," said Kate. "Having finished at his previous parish at the end of October, Mr Neep was spending November on retreat in a little cottage he owns on the Isle of Wight. That's where the attacker struck, hitting his head with a blunt instrument, throwing him down the stairs and locking the door."

"That's more of a retreat than he bargained for," said Hector.

"When he came round, he survived on his cellar's store of home-made beer and jam." Kate grimaced at the thought. "Luckily, the local postman noticed Mr Neep's mail piling up, while his car hadn't moved from the drive, and he called the police. Thanks to that postie's vigilance, Mr Neep lived to tell the tale, but it may take him a while to recover."

"Poor Mr Neep," said Hector.

I smiled. "Now there's a phrase I never thought I'd hear you say."

Kate turned to me for the first time. "I'm sorry, where are my manners? Who are you, dear? Someone else I don't know."

Hector put his arm protectively about my shoulders. "This is Sophie Sayers, Kate. May Sayers's great-niece. She moved into May's old cottage while you were down under, and now she works for me – with me – in the bookshop."

Although he'd slightly redeemed himself with that 'colleague not employee' correction, I still felt disappointed that his first impulse hadn't been to introduce me as his girlfriend.

"Sophie, this is Katherine Blake, chair of the PCC. She's also my godmother, Kate. You know, the one I told you about who helped me refit the shop? She's been in Australia for the last six months, visiting family."

Kate shivered and pulled her coat around her. "It looks like I picked the wrong six months to go to Australia. I'm getting two winters in a row instead of two summers."

Hector took her arm. "Come indoors and warm up with some punch, and we'll tell you all about the excitement that you've missed."

With glasses charged from the punchbowl, the three of us retreated to the vicar's study. The floor was covered in coats – it looked like the guys' dressing room – but the room was free of people. We added our coats to the pile and closed the door for peace and privacy. Katherine seated herself at the vicar's writing desk, while Hector and I settled down on the small sofa. She riffled through the pile of papers on the desktop, which included a few spare invitations to the fireworks party, discarded because the vicar had made a spelling mistake or a crossing out part way through.

She held up one of the cards to show us. "Good Lord, is that his handwriting? Hector, have you no books on graphology in that shop of yours? You really must get in that one I read about in *Woman's Wisdom* magazine. From that article, I could have told you that this is the handwriting of someone who is deeply disturbed." Shuddering, she set it back on the desk, turning it face down as if to curb its power.

"I'm afraid Mr Vance was an impostor all right. But it seems the diocese made it too easy for him to waltz in and pose as the new vicar, what with the vicarage being provided furnished. And they never bothered disconnecting the water or electricity, in case the Bishop wanted to put anyone else up here before the new man arrived. I suspect they may even have left the Reverend Murray's spare key under the flowerpot by the door in its usual hiding place. Why can't people be more original with their secret key stores?"

From the way Hector shifted uncomfortably in his seat, I guessed where he kept his key.

"All Vance needed to do was to pitch up with his own robes, which you can easily buy from an ecclesiastical outfitter, and take his cues from the prayer book in the church. It's like a ready-made script for fake vicars."

"What did he live on, I wonder, when he wouldn't have had access to the real Mr Neep's salary?" asked Hector. "Surely the diocese wouldn't have started paying it yet, as he wasn't due to join the parish for a few weeks."

"Produce from the vicarage vegetable garden?" said Kate. "There's certainly no shortage of apples."

I suspected he'd had his fair share of beans too.

Hector picked up an old oak money box from the floor beneath the desk and turned it over. The hinged flap underneath dropped open.

"The church roof fund collection box. No wonder he was paying Tommy for odd jobs in coppers. Although if Vance had stolen the real Mr Neep's identity, he probably had access to his bank account too."

He got up and started opening the desk drawers until he found what he was looking for: bank cards, a cheque book, driving licence, passport, all in the name of the Reverend Philip Neep. There was a sheet of paper on which Vance appeared to have been practising Mr Neep's signature without much success.

Hector checked the passport photo and raised his eyebrows in astonishment. "Good Lord, they do look alike. I guess that explains why Septimus Vance chose Neep as his victim. He was someone he could easily pass for, especially when he was about to move to a new area where no-one would know him – except you, Kate, and the Bishop. I suspect he may have been watching Neep and planning his ghastly act for some time. I wonder how he knew about him."

"Perhaps he'd spotted him by chance in a wedding photograph in a magazine," said Kate. "Vicars officiate at hundreds of weddings, and people are always sharing wedding photos in magazines, and not just the posh society ones either. He might easily have seen one in a doctor's or dentist's waiting room, or someone else might have spotted it and shown it to him."

I tried to piece the chain of events together in chronological order, but had trouble getting past the awful vision of Vance's ambush on the real Mr Neep. "It must have been a very odd experience for Mr Neep to find himself being attacked by someone so similar to himself in appearance. Talk about being your own worst enemy."

Hector had a literary spin to add. "It's like something out of the old doppelganger myth, which dictates that if you ever meet your double, you die."

"Is that another episode from *Grimm's Fairy Tales*?" I asked him.

He shook his head. "No, but Hans Christian Anderson wrote about a doppelganger in his story 'The Shadow'. And many writers have returned to the same theme over the years. Look at Oscar Wilde and Dorian Gray, for example."

I'd heard of Oscar Wilde, of course, but I never knew he had a double.

"I recall Goethe wrote about a doppelganger experience in his autobiography," added Kate, "although his personal encounter was more positive."

It seemed Kate didn't just read magazines. I was starting to feel out of my depth. There's only so much surreptitious googling a girl can do in the middle of a conversation.

Then an even more frightening idea occurred to me. "Kate, what do you think Vance would have done if you'd turned up sooner - or the Bishop, come to that – and, being the only one in the village who'd ever met Neep, spotted that he was an imposter? My goodness, it could have been you under the bonfire with Simon Yardley!"

Hector tried to reassure Kate. "If the similarity was that strong, there was a good chance you wouldn't have noticed, having met him only once. I expect you'd have been perfectly safe."

Kate shook her head slowly, her eyes widening in realisation. "Oh no, I'd have spotted the difference straight away. You see, there's one small detail that Vance wouldn't have been able to fake. The real Reverend Neep has six fingers on his right hand. I don't think he'd really thought it through. I prefer to believe that than to assume he was going to bump off anyone who rumbled him."

She took the collection box from Hector and closed the flap with a loud clunk, as if to draw a line under the episode. A sad look came in to her eye. "What a tragic waste of a man's life."

I wasn't going to let that go unremarked. "But even if he didn't murder his wife before he came here, he almost certainly attempted to murder the real Mr Neep, drugged Simon Yardley, then tried to kill him and place the blame on Billy."

Kate raised a hand in caution. "Innocent until proven guilty," she said, before adding brightly,

"Not that we haven't all wanted to murder Billy now and again."

Then I remembered she knew nothing about the rest of Vance's antics, so I gave her the potted version. "He's been horrible to everyone ever since he arrived, making out that we were doing the work of the devil by celebrating Halloween. He compared Wendlebury Barrow to Sodom and Gomorrah."

I expected Kate to laugh at that, but she remained serious. "That was probably a coping mechanism for dealing with unresolved guilt and grief about his late wife. I think it's called displacement."

"Which magazine did you glean that theory from?" asked Hector, teasingly.

Kate suppressed a smile. "Well, I still think he's more to be pitied than blamed.

I had to admire her powers of forgiveness. I thought for a moment.

"I wonder whether he prayed for his wife at the All Souls' Day service? If he did, I hope it brought him comfort."

Her charitable attitude, like Joshua's, was infectious.

We fell silent for a moment. Then Kate set down her empty glass on the vicar's desk and rose from her chair.

"Well, I suppose I'd better get down to sorting this muddle out tomorrow. We must restore the vicarage to order for when the real Mr Neep joins us, but I'm not sure that will be any time soon. He might even have to retire, if he's left with any lasting damage. Goodness knows what the Bishop will say when he hears about it all." She clapped her hands decisively. "But don't you worry, dears, you run along and join the party. If you'll excuse me for a moment, I'll stay here to make a couple of quick phone calls."

She patted my shoulder companionably. "Lovely to meet you, Sophie dear. I can see the family resemblance now that we're indoors under the light. May Sayers was a dear lady and is much missed. I'm glad Hector's found you."

I was starting to like this lady a lot.

40 The Last Rocket

Hector and I left Kate in the study and headed for
the spacious drawing room, in which it seemed half
the village was intent on partying into the night.
People of all ages were piled on to sofas and
sprawled on the rugs by the fireplace, chatting and
laughing and exchanging their versions of the events
of the evening. When Kate joined us a few minutes
later, they all turned to wave and cheer, obviously
delighted to welcome her back from her long
holiday. She plunged into their midst, hugging and
kissing people and shaking outstretched hands,
before making her way to the bay window which was
filled with a baby grand piano. Casting aside the
hymn book on the music stand, Kate made herself
comfortable on the piano stool, raised her hands to
play, and then paused for a moment, before reaching
into her pocket.

"Sorry, my phone just went ping. Excuse me a
moment, folks." She flipped open its case to read a
message, then looked up to cast the broadest of
smiles around the room.

"Good news, my friends. Given the unfortunate
indisposition of the real Mr Neep, the Bishop has
persuaded the Reverend Murray to come out of

retirement for a little while to fill the void. So we'll be celebrating Advent with our dear old friend once more."

A roar of approval went around the room, while Kate snapped her phone case shut and slipped it back in her pocket. Perhaps there weren't as many Jedis in the village as Ella feared.

Hector raised his voice so I could hear him over the clamour. "I think you'll like the Reverend Murray rather better than the Reverend Neep."

I smiled. "I think I will. I look forward to meeting him."

Only Carol, squeezed into an armchair with Billy, looked disappointed. Remembering there was also a Mrs Murray, I renewed my resolve to find Carol a more suitable partner by Christmas.

Then Kate poised her hands dramatically over the keyboard, pausing till the room fell silent, before launching into a rollicking rendition of 'Let's Go Fly A Kite' from *Mary Poppins*, playing from memory, and making a singsong inevitable.

Putting his arm around my shoulders, Hector drew me back into the relative quiet of the hall.

"Well done, Hector. Without you, Vance might have got away with it."

He allowed me to give him a congratulatory hug, then tightened his hold on me.

"It's not all down to me, you know. You're the one who remembered what Tommy had said about Neep's books all looking the same, otherwise that crucial evidence might have been lost for ever. And but for your observation of those lime green socks, Yardley of the Yard would have breathed his last by

276

now. You're the one who saved a life tonight, not me."

I leaned against him, suddenly exhausted.

"What I don't get, Hector, is why Vance brought all those copies of his book with him. I mean, if he had stolen Neep's identity, didn't they rather give the game away?"

Hector shrugged. "Vanity? Delusion? Maybe he really did think he'd written a good book, and couldn't bring himself to destroy all traces of it until he absolutely had to. Once he recognised me, even though I didn't remember him, he must have realised he had no choice. He couldn't have picked a less suspicious time to incinerate his books than on Bonfire Night."

"Yes, but with the whole village watching?"

"I didn't say he wasn't also stupid. Maybe he thought he was – dare I say it – fireproof?"

I forced a grin, though all I wanted to do now was find a space to sit quietly alone – or, at least, alone with Hector. I looked up at him.

"To be honest, I think I've had enough excitement for one evening. Do you think it would be terribly rude if I left the party now?"

He released me from the hug. "No, not at all. Let me fetch our coats and I'll walk you home."

I let out a little laugh. "Oh, Hector, really? It's not like we're in the middle of some big city. This is Wendlebury Barrow. I'll be perfectly safe on my own, I'm sure."

"Tell that to Yardley of the Yard."

I took his point.

277

Only as he was helping me on with my coat did I realise how stupid I'd been almost to have missed the opportunity for a midnight stroll alone with Hector on Fireworks Night. What could be more romantic?

Hand in hand, we slipped quietly out of the front door unnoticed and headed up the path to the High Street where all was still. I walked as slowly as I could to make our journey last as long as possible. I hoped Hector planned to walk me all the way back to my house, rather than just as far as his shop. That way our time alone together would last twice as long. I wondered whether to invite him in for coffee if he did, and then remembered I'd run out of coffee.

"Have you left something at the vicarage?" asked Hector, stopping in his tracks beside me.

"No. Why?"

"You were going so slowly I thought you were about to go back the other way."

I shook my head, then shivered a little. I wished I'd worn a hat and scarf. We'd been warm enough in the crowds around the bonfire, but out in the open it was chilly. I huffed a big puff of steam to check the temperature, half-expecting my breath to precipitate into a shower of snow.

"Cold?" asked Hector, slipping his arm around my shoulders. Suddenly glowing, I put my arm around his waist. When he hugged me closer and planted a kiss on my hair, I reached my other arm across his tummy. Soon we were walking along so entwined and in step that we'd have stood a good chance of winning a three-legged race. I made a mental note to suggest one for the next Village Show.

Too quickly, we reached Hector's House. Hector guided us to a halt in front of the shop window. The display already looked strangely dated with its small Action Man guy on top of its cellophane bonfire. Carol had done a wonderful job on his tiny outfit, a purple velveteen suit trimmed with the lace edging salvaged from one of her mother's old cotton handkerchiefs.

"We'd better redo the window first thing tomorrow," said Hector. "After tonight's events, that looks in decidedly poor taste."

"I presume next up will be a Christmas display?"

"No, first we'll have a week of war poetry and poppies, in the run-up to Remembrance Day. Then Christmas-lite, building up slowly with Christmas cookery books, how-to books on present-making, that sort of thing. We'll leave the Christmas tree and fairy lights till Advent. If people want the full works sooner, they can go down to Slate Green. They've been displaying all that stuff since about August anyway. My shop, my rules."

"You're a very bossy boss," I said. I only meant to tease, but he looked suddenly serious.

"Your boss? Is that how you still think of me? I'm sorry, Sophie. You know now why I am so cautious in relationships. But let's not go through all that again. How about we throw caution to the wind, and you come up to my flat for a cup of coffee?"

I wrinkled my nose. "I don't know, I'm still enjoying the after-effects of the punch."

He laughed. "I'll remind you of that when you're clutching your head tomorrow and downing paracetamol. How about a drop of brandy instead?"

If he'd asked me to come upstairs for a glass of drain cleaner, I'd have said yes, and we both knew it.

I wondered why Hector had never invited me into his flat before, when I'd been working in the shop beneath it for the past six months. Was he hiding some dark secret? A mad wife in the attic? A shrine to Celeste? No, I was being silly. He probably just needed a little man cave away from the very public arena of the shop – the bookseller's equivalent of a shed. One way or another, whatever lay inside was Hector's private space.

We skirted around the shop front to the side door that led to the flat. Hector stooped to extract his door key from beneath a big pot of bronze chrysanthemums beside the doorstep, unlocked the door, and told me to go up the stairs ahead of him while he found a new hiding place for the key.

I climbed the wooden staircase, my footsteps muted by a crimson Persian runner, and gently pushed open the door at the top, which gave on to the living room. I stood in the doorway to survey the decor. The room resembled the lounge of a gentleman's club, with dark green winged leather armchairs and matching sofa arranged around a mahogany coffee table piled with books and newspapers. A shaggy cream rug looked like a pressed Himalayan yak, while sturdy tapestry cushions added colour, as did a scarlet cashmere blanket draped over the back of the sofa. In the open fireplace, a log fire was set ready to blaze the minute

Hector put a flame to it. Squatting on the stone hearth stood a tubby bottle of brandy, ready to absorb the fire's heat, and a pair of crystal balloon glasses waiting to receive a splash of its warming nectar.

But it wasn't the ruggedly masculine furniture that most impressed me, nor the promise of a fireside nightcap, nor even the evidence of Hector's confidence that he would not be returning home alone that night. Instead it was something that stood on the neatly ordered top of the huge antique oak writing desk under the front window. I recognised the person in the solitary silver photo frame as Virginia Woolf. Then I realised it wasn't Virgina Woolf at all, but me, snapped unawares in profile on the day of the Village Show, where I'd been dressed as the great author on the Wendlebury Writers' float. Hector must have photographed me, taken me back to his flat and put me in pride of place on his desk.

Next to the photo stood a small crystal vase of sky-blue forget-me-nots – fake fabric ones, of course, because this was November. But that didn't matter.

"You've got the wrong colour eyes for Virginia Woolf," he'd said me when I'd announced my alter ego for the Show. "Hers were grey. Yours are forget-me-not blue."

By this time Hector had reached the top of the stairs and was standing behind me, his hands gently resting on my waist. "So, what do you think of my flat?"

With one hand, he swept my loose hair over my shoulder and kissed the back of my neck.

I leaned against him. "I think it's lovely."

Taking my hand, he led me over to the sofa, then he crossed to the fireplace, knelt down, and struck a match to the fire. It began to crackle pleasingly beneath his touch. He opened the bottle of brandy, poured a little into each of the two glasses, set them on the coffee table, and came to sit beside me on the sofa. Then he picked up the remote control from the coffee table and pressed play. As the overture of Handel's Firework Music reverberated around the room, he settled back and drew me closer to him.

"Now," he said softly, "let the fireworks commence."

Coming Soon

Further down the High Street, a few hundred yards from where Sophie and Hector were getting beyond the sparkler stage, past The Bluebird and the village shop and the village green, a battered white camper van had just pulled up outside May Sayers's cottage. A tall, gangly man with the thick, wild hair of a Viking got out, pushed open the gate, and strode up to knock on the front door. He waited a few moments, then knocked again impatiently.

With a theatrical sigh, he stepped back to look up to the first floor of the cottage. The curtains had not been closed, so he assumed Sophie must be away for the weekend. Or perhaps she was out somewhere locally – babysitting, probably. She'd never get a date in a place like this.

He trudged back down the front path, let the gate clank shut behind him and slid open the side door of his van. He clambered up inside, reached his sleeping bag down from the shelf, and slammed the door shut.

Weary and aching after his long drive from Bremen, he couldn't wait to crash out. Still, he thought, that was the joy of having a camper van. Unexpected developments didn't matter. He could just turn in for the night here and wait to see what the morning would bring.

He hoped it would bring Sophie. She'd soon help him get the job of Director for the Wendlebury Players, as advertised on her bookshop's website, to tide him over while his own company was resting. He didn't suppose it would pay much, but his living expenses would be pretty negligible, when he shacked up with Sophie again. He could probably persuade Sophie to pay for his van repairs, too, now that she was a rich householder.

Yes, Sophie. Good old Sophie. He didn't foresee any problem there. Since she'd moved to Wendlebury, Damian had begun to realise that he could do a lot worse.

More Sophie Sayers Village Mysteries for You to Enjoy

If you enjoyed this book, you might like to know that the next in the Sophie Sayers Village Mysteries, *Murder in the Manger*, will be published on 6 November 2017 and is now available to pre-order.

And if you missed the start of the series, it's *Best Murder in Show*.

Murder in the Manger – A Christmas Special

When Sophie Sayers volunteers to write a traditional Christmas nativity play, she finds the task attracts far more trouble than she'd anticipated - not least the strange woman who accuses the entire village of murder in the middle of the performance.

Nor has she reckoned on her ex-boyfriend Damian pitching up as the play's director, just as her romance with local bookseller Hector is finally taking off. Will Hector's jealousy scupper their new relationship? And can Sophie prevent Damian breaking the heart of lonely shopkeeper Carol who takes him in as a lodger?

As she tries to unravel all their secrets, Sophie's imagination goes into overdrive. Can you solve the mystery of the strange woman's missing baby before she does?

For fans of cosy mysteries everywhere, *Murder in the Manger* is the perfect Christmas read, making you laugh out loud at the eccentricities of English village life and warming your heart with its traditional community values.

Acknowledgments

For making this book very much better than it would have been if I was left to my own devices, I would like to thank the following wonderful people:

Alison Jack, my editor, who always manages to find and resolve my mistakes without denting my confidence

David Penny for planting the idea of a live person in the bonfire (he will forever be in my head "Penny for the Guy"), for generously sharing his expertise in crime and thriller writing, and for his heartening confidence in my ability

Orna Ross for her encouragement, enthusiasm and wise guidance as a beta reader

Belinda Pollard for her wisdom and warmth as a beta reader with an Australian perspective (the book she's now writing about beta reading will be a must-read for any author)

Lucienne Boyce, for her brilliance at beta reading, in particular her eye for detail, for the ridiculous and for her sense of decency (she's saved my characters more than once from doing something in dubious taste)

Richard Bradburn for suggesting "Murder at the Vicarage" when I needed to cite a play that featured a vicar

Rachel Lawston of Lawston Design for her much-admired cover design for this book and for the whole Sophie Sayers Village Mysteries series

Pauline Setterfield of Hawkesbury's Parochial Church Council for advice about All Souls' Day

I would also like to thank my family, friends and neighbours for their encouragement and enthusiasm, especially my parents, and my sister Mandy Gooding; neighbours Emma Barker, Marina Pogose, Chris Taylor; old schoolfriends Aaren Purcell, Elizabeth Scahill, Jane Martin, and Susanne Mitchell (and her daughter Madalen); American friends Becky Brain and Shay Tressa DeSimone; and my author friends around the world, especially members of the Alliance of Independent Authors.

Special thanks to booksellers everywhere, especially the staff of the Anthology in Cheltenham, the Yellow-Lighted Bookshop in Tetbury and Nailsworth, the Cotswold Book Room in Wotton-under-Edge, and Foyles' Bristol branch, for their politeness and diplomacy to the Mr Neeps of this world, as well as to me

All your support and encouragement makes my day and drives me to write my next book. Thank you.

Debbie Young

About the Author

Debbie Young writes warm, witty, feel-good fiction inspired by life in the English village where she lives with her husband and daughter.

Her Sophie Sayers Village Mystery series of seven stories cataloguing the course of a year in the village of Wendlebury Barrow will be published during 2017 and 2018.

She also publishes a new themed collection of short stories every year, such as *Marry in Haste*, *Quick Change* and *Stocking Fillers*. Her short stories also feature in many anthologies.

She is frequently invited to read her work or speak at public events and has performed at events such as the Cheltenham Literature Festival and Stroud Short Stories. She is founder and director of the Hawkesbury Upton Literature Festival.

A regular contributor to two local community magazines, the award-winning *Tetbury Advertiser* and the *Hawkesbury Parish News*, she has published two collections of her columns, *Young by Name* and *All Part of the Charm*, which offer insight into her own life in a small Cotswold village very similar to Sophie Sayers' Wendlebury Barrow.

Keep up to date with news of Debbie Young's book news and events via her website, www.authordebbieyoung.com. You can also follower her on Twitter at @DebbieYoungBN.

Printed in Poland
by Amazon Fulfillment
Poland Sp. z o.o., Wrocław